EUGENE ONEGIN

ALEXANDER SERGEEVICH PUSHKIN was born in Moscow in 1799 into an old aristocratic family. As a schoolboy he demonstrated a precocious talent for verse and was recognized as a poetic prodigy by prominent older writers. In 1817 he received a nominal appointment in the government service, but for the most part he led a dissipated life in the capital while he continued to produce much highly polished light verse. His narrative poem, *Ruslan and Lyudmila* (publ. 1820), brought him widespread fame and secured his place as the leading figure in Russian poetry. At about the same time a few mildly seditious verses led to his banishment from the capital. During this so-called 'southern exile', he composed several narrative poems and began his novel in verse, *Eugene Onegin*. As a result of further conflicts with state authorities he was condemned to a new period of exile at his family's estate of Mikhailovskoe. There he wrote some of his finest lyric poetry, completed his verse drama *Boris Godunov*, and continued work on *Eugene Onegin*. He was still in enforced absence from the capital when the Decembrist Revolt of 1825 took place. Although several of his friends were among those executed or imprisoned, he himself was not implicated in the affair, and in 1826 he was pardoned by the new Czar Nicholas I and permitted to return to Moscow. By the end of the decade, as he sought to become a truly professional writer, he turned increasingly to prose composition. In the especially fruitful autumn of 1830, while stranded at his estate of Boldino, he completed *Eugene Onegin*, wrote a major collection of prose stories (*The Tales of Belkin*), and composed his experimental 'Little Tragedies'. In 1831, he married Natalya Goncharova and sought to put his personal and professional affairs on a more stable footing. The rest of his life, however, was plagued by financial and marital woes, by the hostility of literary and political enemies, and by the younger generation's dismissal of his recent work. His literary productivity diminished, but in the remarkable 'second Boldino autumn' of 1833 he produced both his greatest prose tale, *The Queen of Spades*, and a last poetic masterpiece, *The Bronze Horseman*. In 1836 he completed his only novel-length work in prose, *The Captain's Daughter*. Beleaguered by numerous adversaries and enraged by anonymous letters containing attacks on his honour, he was driven in 1837 to challenge an importunate admirer of his wife to a duel. The contest took place on 27 February, and two days later, the poet died from his wounds.

JAMES E. FALEN is Professor of Russian at the University of Tennessee, where he teaches nineteenth- and twentieth-century Russian literature and Russian language. He is the author of *Isaac Babel: Russian Master of the Short Story* (University of Tennessee Press, 1974) and has published translations of lyric and dramatic verse by Alexander Pushkin. He is currently working on translations of twentieth-century Russian poetry.

OXFORD WORLD'S CLASSICS

====

ALEXANDER PUSHKIN

Eugene Onegin
A Novel in Verse

====

Translated with an Introduction and Notes by
JAMES E. FALEN

Oxford   New York
OXFORD UNIVERSITY PRESS

Oxford University Press, Great Clarendon Street, Oxford OX2 6DP

Oxford New York

Athens Auckland Bangkok Bogotá Buenos Aires Calcutta
Cape Town Chennai Dar es Salaam Delhi Florence Hong Kong Istanbul
Karachi Kuala Lumpur Madrid Melbourne Mexico City Mumbai
Nairobi Paris São Paulo Singapore Taipei Tokyo Toronto Warsaw
and associated companies in Berlin Ibadan

Oxford is a registered trade mark of Oxford University Press

First published as a World's Classics paperback 1995
Reissued as an Oxford World's Classics paperback 1998

British Library Cataloguing in Publication Data

Data available

Library of Congress Cataloging in Publication Data
Pushkin, Aleksandr Sergeevich, 1799–1837.
[Evgeniĭ Onegin. English]
Eugene Onegin : a novel in verse / Alexander Pushkin ; translated
with an introduction and notes by James E. Falen.
Includes bibliographical references.
I. Falen, James E., 1935– . II. Title. III. Series.
PG3347.E8F35 1995 891.73'3—dc20 94-45634
ISBN 0-19-283899-7

3 5 7 9 10 8 6 4 2

Printed in Great Britain by
Cox & Wyman , Reading, Berkshire

CONTENTS

NOTE ON THE TRANSLATION

If art holds a mirror up to nature, it frequently does so—as in this masterpiece of Pushkin's—by first directing that mirror at other works of art. The world of *Eugene Onegin* derives perhaps as much from Western European literary antecedents and traditions as it does from its author's Russia, and in doing so it provides a paradoxical picture of life mimicking art. The literary translator, in seeking to participate in this international colloquy, holds, as it were, yet another mirror up to these already doubled or tripled mirrors. It is a devilish and tricky business, this game in a house of mirrors, this effort to catch and reflect elusive reflections. There are occasions when the translator, however carefully he tries to grip his own mirror by its edges so as not to smudge the glass, will inadvertently allow his hands to enter the picture and thus obscure the view.

In attempting to reproduce poetry, the verbal art most closely tied to its native language and the most susceptible to distortion in the transfer to another, the translator faces particularly vexing difficulties. Verse, perhaps, can be translated; great poetry is something else. Russian and English poetry do not look, sound, or behave very much alike; and by choosing to work on Pushkin's poem, in which the sheer beauty of sound is so vital a part of its effect and in which all the expressive resources of the Russian language are on masterful display, the translator may find himself casting an uneasy eye at Robert Frost's cautionary definition of poetry as 'what gets lost in translation'. All he can do, having begun, is keep to his task, reassuring himself that both Russian and English, after all, assemble consonants and vowels into sounds and words, into beauty and sense.

Pushkin's long poem has had some seven English translations prior to this one (the more thorough Germans seem to have produced about twelve), and yet it has continued to be regarded by many as a classic instance of the untranslatable work. Vladimir Nabokov has argued that a literal rendering of Pushkin's sentences is about the best that can be achieved or even honestly attempted; that any translation that retains the original's metre and rhyme, since it cannot be faithful to the work's exact meaning, will necessarily result in a mere paraphrase. In his own translation of the novel, which he proudly labelled a 'pony', he shunned, accordingly, both metre and rhyme and gave us a version at once marvellously accurate and rather peculiar, most of its poetry resident in the accompanying commentary rather than in the translation itself. Pushkin, one has to say, loses where Nabokov gains. And of course a 'literal' version is, in the end, no less unfaithful to its model than a rhymed and metred one: in place of a work whose austere and harmonious shape is an essential part of its effect, it gives us something ill-proportioned and flaccid, a kind of 'formal paraphrase' that seems bland and inert where the original is expressive and alive. But the translator's dilemma doesn't lie, really, in choosing between faithfulness to form and faithfulness to meaning, for in fact neither of these goals, even separately, is attainable. In the transfer of a work from one language to another there are no exact correspondences to be found— neither in the meanings and histories of words nor in the intricacies and effects of forms. This very tendency of ours to divide a work of art into separate categories of form and content not only gives a false view of a work's complex nature but also poses the problem of literary translation in a false light.

Confronted with an evident inability to render a work faithfully in either its absolute form or its total sense, the translator, it would seem, faces an impossible task and is condemned by the very nature of his enterprise to an act of compromise and betrayal. The only solution, it seems to me, is for the translator to try to view the work not as a hopeless dichotomy but as a unified whole and to try to be faithful, in some mysterious spirit, to this vision of wholeness. In the result, perhaps we can honour, if nothing else, the poor

INTRODUCTION

Alexander Pushkin (1799–1837) is the poet and writer whom Russians regard as both the source and the summit of their literature. Not only is he revered, like Shakespeare in the English tradition or Goethe in the German, as the supreme national poet, but he has become a kind of cultural myth, an iconic figure around whom a veritable cult of idolatry has been fashioned. This exalted status that Pushkin has been accorded in his own land has been something of a disservice to the living reality of his works, and it contrasts oddly with the more modest reputation that Pushkin has secured abroad. To many non-native readers of Russian literature the panegyrics of his compatriots seem excessive, and indeed, in their eyes, Pushkin has been somewhat overshadowed by the great Russian writers who came after him. They do not comprehend why these writers themselves generally grant him the first and highest place in their pantheon of artistic geniuses. For those who do not read Pushkin in his own language, the situation remains perplexing and the questions persist: just who is he and why, almost without exception, do the most perceptive of his compatriots regard him as one of the world's greatest artists?

Within the Russian tradition the scope of Pushkin's achievement is essentially clear and well established. He is unarguably a figure of protean dimensions, the author in his own right of a formidable and enduring body of work and at the same time the seminal writer whose example has nourished, enriched, and in large part directed all subsequent literature in the language. He came of age at a historical moment when the Russian literary language, after a century or so of imitation of foreign models, had been roughly shaped and readied for the hand of an original genius. Pushkin was to fulfil that role.

He began his career in an era when both the writers and the readers of literature belonged almost exclusively to the limited milieu of aristocratic society and at a time when poetry rather than prose was the dominant mode for high literature. Well read in both the ancient classics and in Western European literature, especially French literature of the seventeenth and eighteenth centuries, Pushkin was the most dazzlingly talented member of a younger generation of writers who were attempting, under the banner of romanticism, to reform and invigorate the language and the styles of poetry. If Pushkin's early work (he began composing as a schoolboy prodigy) was facile and conventional, consisting mainly of light verse suitable for the literary salons of the day (frothy Epicurean pieces, witty epigrams, album verse), it already displayed an impressive plasticity of language that was new in Russian literature; and quite soon he exhibited a mastery of virtually all the poetic genres and styles known to the writers of his era. The eventual range of his creativity was enormous, embracing not only all the prevailing forms of lyric verse (which he reshaped into his own freer medium of expression), but including brilliant examples of narrative verse as well. He also achieved stunning success in poetry based on the idioms and themes of Russian folklore, and he experimented fascinatingly in the field of verse drama, both on a large Shakespearian scale and in intensely concentrated, minimalist studies of human passions. He is, in sum, a poet of astonishing versatility. Possessed of a uniquely supple linguistic instrument, he is the master of an apparently effortless naturalness, a seamless blend of appropriate sound, sense, and feeling.

During the last decade of his life, when literary activity was being democratized and commercialized, and when a larger, more broadly based readership was emerging, Pushkin turned increasingly to prose, which was fast outdistancing poetry in popularity, though it had yet to achieve the same high level of excellence attained by Russian verse. Pushkin's prose fiction, which is characterized by an unusual terseness and precision of expression, includes several masterpieces in the short-story form, one completed historical novel (as well as the beginnings of several others), and a number of unfinished drafts of a contemporary social novel. He also made significant contributions to Russian culture as a journalist, as a literary critic and editor, as an accomplished letter-writer, and as a gifted, if amateur, historian. He became in effect Russia's first complete man of letters.

All his creative life Pushkin suffered from the indignities and impositions of an autocratic state: exile in his youth, the frustrations of police surveillance and a grossly interfering censorship in his later years, the constant and onerous obligations of government service, and the continuing humiliation of having to rely on imperial favour. In an effort to secure his independence from such state control over his affairs he gave his political allegiance to a kind of 'aristocratic party', seeing in the old Russian landed gentry, the class to which he himself was born, the only viable check on the arbitrary power of the autocracy. This aligned him as well, in a literary sense, with the notion, prevalent among the educated members of 'élite' society, that the writer's appropriate role was that of the gentleman *littérateur*, a view of the artist that probably hindered Pushkin in his effort, during the last decade of his life, to transform himself into a truly free and independent professional writer. He never succeeded, finally, in escaping from either the constraints of court pressure or his own persistent allegiance to a fading aristocratic culture. His further development as an artist was abruptly terminated by his death in a duel at the age of 38.

In both his poetry and his prose Pushkin was a profound innovator. He brought to its successful conclusion the revolt against the tenets of French neoclassicism, which, with its rigid divisions and classifications of genres, had dominated the literature of the eighteenth and early nineteenth centuries. Life, in Pushkin's view, was wilder and more various than these conventions would allow, and, although he always retained a rather classical respect for balance and proportion in art, he introduced into his native literature a new sense of artistic freedom. His formal experiments encouraged a vigorous inventiveness in the writers who followed him, and his modernization of the diction and syntax of literary texts with infusions of living contemporary speech pointed the way to a perennial renewal of the literary language. In the area of literary subject-matter as well his influence was far-reaching: he introduced a host of suggestive themes that later writers would explore more fully, and he greatly enlarged the cast of characters in serious literature. No topic or person lay beyond the reach of his interest; his poetry and prose are filled with life's essential concerns and activities—with love, work, art, history, politics, and nature; with all the mundane trivia of everyday existence and with the more rarefied realm of dreams and thoughts. He virtually created and shaped modern Russian literature and in countless ways determined the course it would follow after him.

Those who seek labels have made numerous attempts to define and categorize this astonishing writer. He has been called variously a romantic and a realist, the poet of freedom and the bard of Russia's imperium; he has been dubbed in political terms a radical, a liberal, and a conservative, a revolutionary critic of the Czarist regime and its loyal defender. Persuasive arguments can and have been made in support of each of these characterizations, but a poet of genius always in the end evades our efforts to tame and contain him.

This brief assessment of Pushkin's place in Russian literature, although it provides a reasonably accurate recital of established critical views, ignores certain anomalies and paradoxes that are part of the Pushkin story. Rather curiously, for example, all the prolific and prodigious achievement of this 'father of Russian literature' was the work of a man whose chief public mask in his own day was that of a gadfly and wastrel. Disciplined in his art, he was often irresponsible and profligate in his social behaviour. There was about him, as the reminiscences of contemporaries observe, something of the eternal schoolboy and prankster, a bit of the renegade always at odds with the respectable adult world. For several years he played the roles of dandy or bohemian; he loved to shock with outlandish dress or outrageous behaviour, and he enjoyed flirting recklessly with the dangers of a dissolute and dissident life. Upon leaving school he put on, briefly, the mask of political rebel and quite consciously provoked, with several courageous poems of liberal sentiment, the displeasure of the emperor, for which he was punished with removal from the centres of Russian culture and power. Even then, in banishment, he courted further punitive action from the authorities by circulating verse of blasphemous, if humorous, content.

Exile seems to have been a defining experience of Pushkin's young manhood. He deeply resented his enforced absence from the social scene, yet he gained through his distance from the centre of events a clearer vision of the society he craved to rejoin. When he was permitted, eventually, to reside once again in St Petersburg and Moscow, he quickly set about to re-establish his nonconformist credentials, indulging once more in a dissipated style of life, although it now seemed less appropriate to his advancing years. Even after his marriage (at almost 32), when he had ostensibly settled down, he continued to provoke outrage, antagonism, and even ridicule with his endless literary feuds, his increasingly touchy pride in his ancient lineage, and his utter contempt for the circles of the court. Yet another cause for the contradictory impulses of his spirit was the black African strain in his ancestry, a heritage that he saw as both a source of uniqueness and a mark of his alienation from the society whose acceptance he simultaneously rejected and craved. At times he revelled in his 'African strangeness' and spoke of his 'moorish' features as the emblem of an elemental and primordial side of his identity, while on other occasions he lamented the racial characteristics that set him apart from those around him. In any case, whatever his ambivalences, it seems clear that Pushkin relished as well as resented his estrangement from society; and certainly his marginal position in it helped him to see all the triviality and hypocrisy of the *monde*. If he continued to live by its codes, he also studied it keenly as an artist and depicted it matchlessly in his work.

Even by the standards of his time and circle Pushkin's appetite for dissipation was large. He was an inveterate gambler and a famous seducer of women, behaviour that he was reluctant to relinquish, not merely out of a mindless adoption of available social roles, but because of the special powers that he attributed to chance and sensuality in his creative life. His youthful anacreontic verse with its playful eroticism, several narrative poems of refined ribaldry, and his more mature love poetry all testify to a deeply sensual nature; and his passion for gambling figures prominently in some of his finest prose works. He was always fascinated, on behalf of his art, in the play of the fortuitous, in the luck of the draw, in the creative possibilities of life's contingencies. He was willing as man and artist to trust in chance, to submit to it as the mechanism that, while it might condemn him to an outwardly undefined and precarious exist- ence, would also assure his inner artistic freedom and his poetic destiny. Chance, in Pushkin's view, was the servant of the greater thing that he called fate, and his reverence for fate as the ultimate shaper of human destinies haunts his work at almost every stage of his career. Essentially buoyant and optimistic in his youth, perceiving fate as the artist's benign and essential guide, he would never distrust it, not even when later in his life it took on an ominous and threatening aspect. Opposition to the tyranny of human institutions was an essen- tial element in Pushkin's conception of the free artist, but resistance to fate, he believed, was a perilous course of action for any individual; for himself he was convinced it was the surest way to destruction as a poet. These elements of Pushkin's character—his sensuality, his courting of chance, and his trust in fate—are essential clues to his artistic nature and to his conception of creativity. He is an artist for whom personality means little, for whom an ordinary human nature and a mundane existence are the very attributes and signs of the poet who is fully engaged with life and at the same time receptive to the designs of Providence.

The poet for Pushkin is a mysterious being: inspired to

exalted utterance by strange gods, yet remaining at an everyday level the most insignificant of humans, a misfit and outcast. Far from being in *propria persona* a poetic demi-urge, the poet is the instrument and voice of powers beyond the self. This is a conception of the poet that combines elements of both a romantic and an anti-romantic sensibility. It yokes together two disparate images, that of the divinely inspired seer and that of the human misfit. It is a vision, of course, with ancient roots and, in its specifically Russian variant, with links to the native tradition of the 'jurodivy', the wandering 'holy fool' of popular veneration. For Pushkin such an image of the poet provides a justification for asserting at once an enormous arrogance for his art and a fundamental humility toward his gift. And perhaps it helps to explain the peculiar instability and elusiveness of Pushkin's artistic personality, the odd sense his reader has that the author is both palpably present in his work and yet nowhere to be found. We seldom know directly what this author *thinks*, even about seemingly obvious things, and we are made uneasy by this lack of a familiar and reassuring human intelligence. The point is not that Pushkin leaves a great deal to the reader's creativity and perception, though he does, but rather that his genius is to an unusual extent of a peculiarly negative kind. He is that rare artist who possesses to an extreme degree a kind of splendid receptivity, an ability to absorb and embody the very energy of his surroundings, to take into himself with an amazing sympathy all the shapes and colours of the life that he sees and hears and responds to. He may or he may not examine intellectually the life that he describes, he may or he may not admire it or approve of it, but what he *must* do is reveal it, recreate it in its vivacity, display his sheer perception of it, refraining from an easy human judgement.

Pushkin is something of an artistic chameleon, and this is why it is so difficult to define him or to fix on a clear and consistent image of his authorial person and stance. He seems almost to lack a coherent artistic persona; like a chameleon, he seems capable of changing his colours and of adapting to almost any milieu. He is enormously alive to the ephemera of experience, fascinated by everything and everyone: the sublime and the ridiculous; the sacred and the profane; all the roles that people play and every style of behaviour; he is interested equally in the talented and the mediocre, in the articulate and the dumb; in Czars, peasants, soldiers, fops, rakes, society women, vulnerable girls, rascals, villains, and almost anyone else. He wants, if only fleetingly, to capture everything, to absorb it all in his appetite for life—even at the risk of losing himself, or perhaps out of the need to lose himself. And the vision that emerges from this fleeting race through experience is no less perceptive and suggestive than many more lengthy examinations of life. Pushkin's manner of describing phenomena is fleeting and abrupt because he is never sated, never content, never willing to stay in one place; he has to rush on to the next person or thing that catches his eye. His omnivorous curiosity lends a kind of 'lightness' as well as universality to Pushkin's work—a lightness of touch, weight, and illumination. The quality is legendary in descriptions of Pushkin's art, but it can be mistaken for superficiality. Our elusive author appears to take few things seriously (not excluding himself) and often poses as a mere 'entertainer'. Entertaining he certainly is, but if we, as readers, are taken in by his ruse and allow ourselves to become inattentive, we are in danger of missing the subtle and hidden aspect of his art.

The effect of lightness, the exceptional clarity that so famously accompanies Pushkin's breadth of interests, goes hand in hand with his vaunted terseness and simplicity, his evident and easy accessibility. But his terseness can be more apparent than real, for his art has the capacity to suggest much in a few spare and simple observations, and his simplicity can be deceptive, screening from the casual reader an art of great sophistication and delicacy. To the foreign reader, especially, Pushkin's qualities of clarity and simplicity can be an impediment to the appreciation of his work; and if the reader has first come to Russian literature through the tormented and profound explorations of

Tolstoy or Dostoevsky, Pushkin's view of the passing scene, filled with a bracing humour as well as grief, may produce a rather strange impression; he is not at all what such a reader has come to expect of a Russian writer. Unlike those two later masters, Pushkin is neither philosopher nor religious thinker, neither didactic moralist nor analytical psychologist. He is both more universal in his sympathies and more modest in his artistic person.

Perhaps, in his final years, this poet of light could not fully adjust to the passing of his youth and the waning of youth's poetic energy. If he would not become a poet of the dark, perhaps he did at the last become the seer of an 'unbearable lightness of being'. In several of his later poems some spectral beast of retribution seems to haunt the poet's mind, along with premonitions of, and even yearnings for, an early death. But the ending in human life is always the same, whereas in great art, as in the plenitude of Pushkin's work, it can at least seem otherwise. Pushkin retained to the last his humility before Providence and he went to his duel and his death completely in character. We cannot, finally, answer the question: who is Pushkin? We can only say with some degree of certainty *what* he is: Russia's most utter artist, its closest thing to the pure poet incarnate, that being who sacrifices all the other possibilities of his human existence to the expression, through language, of life's fascinating variety. The aim of poetry, Pushkin asserted, is poetry itself; the poet emerges from the creative spirit to show us the world and speak of things beyond our normal ken; he is the voice of time's fleeting and intricate fullness.

Central to any consideration of Pushkin's art is his 'novel in verse', *Eugene Onegin*, a work unique in Russian literature and one with few if any parallels outside it. Although it occupies in some respects an isolated and idiosyncratic place in Pushkin's *œuvre*, it is also his most deeply characteristic creation. It was his own favourite among his works and may well be his greatest single contribution to world literature. Despite its considerable literary sophistication and complexity and the fact of its having been written in verse, it may be more accessible to the appreciation of non-Russian readers than most of Pushkin's other work. Almost all of us, even those who are resistant to poetry (especially in translation!), are readers of novels; and Pushkin's long poem, with its stanzas that mimic paragraphs and its verse that seems as natural as familiar prose, subtly entices us by its successful masquerade as a novel. The writer spent some eight years writing it (far longer than he devoted to any other work), and it thus accompanied him through an extended and crucial period of his life. It not only reflects the vital changes that were taking place in Pushkin himself during those years, but it also represents its author's response to a transformation in the general literary climate. By the late 1820s the rage was all for new works in prose rather than poetry, and although Russian literature had as yet produced few prose works of any lasting distinction, writers were eager to answer the demands of the time. Pushkin was among the first of the established authors to respond to the need for a serious prose literature. This change in public taste and Pushkin's effort to respond to it took place in the very years when the writer was composing *Eugene Onegin*. Begun when Pushkin was only 24, still ebullient in his poetic personality and still partially under the sway of his fascination with Byron, it was completed in his thirty-second year, when he was already the author of several prose works of a strongly anti-romantic cast. *Onegin*, as the work's hybrid nature suggests, belongs to a transitional phase in Pushkin's career and constitutes a kind of bridge linking two literary eras. It shows us its author, at the central period of his life, in the very act of crossing that bridge, attempting to transform himself from romantic poet into a novelist who would paint on a large canvas an expansive picture of social reality. Paradoxically *Eugene Onegin*, although written in verse, is the earliest of Pushkin's works to contain a major component of the 'prosaic' in motivation and spirit. This rather complex set of personal and historical factors informs this first great

Russian novel (and arguably the most influential) in a number of crucial ways and provides the ground for its unique flavour and a strangeness that both delights and perplexes the reader.

The work is many things: a stylistic *tour de force*, an examination of human character and of the power in human affairs of cultural phenomena (especially social and artistic conventions), an investigation of the interconnections between literature and life, an autobiography, and an exploration of the creative process itself. It is also, of course, and above all else, incomparable poetry. Highly structured in its use of an unvarying stanzaic form and in its classically balanced design, the work nevertheless conveys an atmosphere of free-flowing spontaneity. Its verse, while observing elegantly the requirements of metre and rhyme, is able at the same time to achieve the rhythm and feel of the most natural and ordinary colloquial speech. Like a discursive prose work, the novel exhibits a wealth of genial, meandering talk and an apparently casual approach to narrative pace. The plot itself is elegantly simple. Treating of the frustrations of love, it deals, as Vladimir Nabokov puts it, 'with the emotions, meditations, acts and destinies of three men: Onegin, the bored fop; Lensky, the minor elegiast; and a stylized Pushkin, Onegin's friend'[1]—and, in a pleasing symmetry, with the affections and fates of three heroines: Tatyana, the shy and bookish provincial maiden; Olga, her beautiful but ordinary younger sister; and Pushkin's mercurial Muse. The action, set in the imperial Russia of the 1820s, begins in a glittering St Petersburg, moves for an extended stay to the bucolic country estate, sojourns for a chapter in Moscow, and then, as if closing a circle, comes to its end in the capital once more. Along its devious narrative route, the novel treats the reader to an engaging and suspenseful story; to lively scenes of city and country life; to portraits of a socially mixed cast of characters; to evocations of nature in its various seasons; and to

---

[1] *Eugene Onegin: A Novel in Verse by Alexander Pushkin, Translated from the Russian with a Commentary* (New York, 1964), iv. 6.

a wealth of authorial digression and commentary, à la Byron or Sterne, on the tale in the telling and on sundry literary, philosophical, and autobiographical matters—all in a shifting play of many moods and tones: lyrical, realistic, parodic, romantic, and ironic.

Much commentary on the work has focused, understandably enough, on its hero and heroine, Onegin and Tatyana, the ill-starred but non-tragic lovers who were to become the proto-types for a host of figures created by later Russian writers. Those critics who approach the text as a realistic novel and who accept its heroes as more or less psychologically plausible representatives of their society, have viewed the two main characters in quite varied and even conflicting ways. To some, Onegin is a victim of his environment, a potentially creative man whose personal fulfilment is frustrated by the limited opportunities available to him in his era. To others he is an anti-hero, an amoral hedonist and misanthropic egoist. Tatyana, though usually regarded in an almost hagiographic light (she is for many Russians the most beloved heroine in their literature), also has a few detractors, readers who see her as an immature woman in whom instinctual drives and vague intuition rather than active intelligence or innate spiritual nobility account for most of her actions. All those critics who attempt such analyses of the characters are confronted by certain puzzling inconsist-encies in their behaviour; in different parts of the novel they seem almost to be different people. A reasonable explanation, not much noted, for the antithetical interpretations the heroes have evoked is that they are dichotomous in their very natures: over the long period of the novel's composition, Pushkin's own artistic values and aims were changing, and it seems quite likely that his characters evolved as well, that his image of them ripened and deepened over that period. There is also a funda-mental, if rich, ambiguity in the author's treatment of Onegin and Tatyana as both character-studies and poetic symbols.

Other critics of the work have taken a more formalist approach, viewing the characters less as real people than as reflections of literary stereotypes. Literary art and language itself, in their view, are always self-referential, uninvolved in any realities supposed to exist outside the work. Such readings also face difficulties and complications. Pushkin's fictional heroes are themselves avid readers of fiction, they construct their identities as much from books as from available social roles. Onegin, in resisting the constrictions of social conventions, adopts the dissident poses of dandy and cynic; but these are only further conventional masks, disguises borrowed from books. Onegin's lack of a solid identity becomes clear to the reader, and to Tatyana within the novel itself, with the realization that he is mostly a congeries of literary affectations, a parody: he has modelled himself on the currently fashionable Byronic type, while at the same time he appears, in Tatyana's vivid literary imagination, as the thrilling hero of a Gothic romance. Pushkin has great satirical fun in playing with these various literary echoes and he has his hero, more empty shell than either rebel or demon, confront his fate not in a romantic-ally primordial wilderness, but in the homely setting of a Russian country estate. Similarly, Tatyana, though less parod-ied by the author (because she is capable of genuine feeling), is composed of a number of literary and cultural personae. To the narrator she contains elements of the 'savage female', a being untouched by civilization's denaturing forces (a fantasy of many male romantic writers); to Onegin, when he first encounters her, she is merely a naïve provincial girl; and by the novel's end she is for both Onegin and her new aristocratic milieu the very embodiment of a successful society hostess and legislatrix. Tatyana too confronts her fate in a kind of literary parody: she discovers the true nature of her hero not by a passage into the dark recesses of a medieval castle, but by reading Onegin's books in his abandoned country house, itself a symbol of the hero's vacancy.

We may note, in order to illustrate one of Pushkin's methods for revealing the power of cultural determinants in his charac-ters' behaviour, the various explanations the narrator gives for

Tatyana's falling in love. We are told that she does so as a 'child of nature', spontaneously and without artificial contrivance; that she falls in love in response to the neighbours' gossip, which has planted the idea in her mind; that it is due to the influence of the epistolary novels she has read; or that it was simply appropriate to her age and social expectations. Having amused his readers with this shrewd undermining of typical romantic attitudes, Pushkin then surprises them and complicates their perceptions of 'truth' by giving a beautifully poetic description of Tatyana as a girl actually in love, with all the restless pain, joy, and dreaminess of her condition. The scene occurs, furthermore, in the wonderfully effective context of Tatyana's conversation with her concerned old nurse, seen in touching and realistic counterpoint to the feverish young girl.

Lensky is yet another figure who derives from books. Creating himself out of his naïve literary readings and aspirations, he becomes a gentle parody of the sentimental romantic poet. What is particularly interesting and somewhat paradoxical, however, is that most of the characters transcend their function as parodies. They are treated by their creator with a sometimes puzzling blend of ironic detachment and sympathetic concern. It is one of the charms of the novel that the author (or at least the narrator) shares at times the viewpoint and attitudes of his most naïve reader.

The narrator constantly intrudes on his story, postponing with his various digressions its progress, speculating on where it might lead, and frequently frustrating his reader's expectations. By exposing the work's contrived 'literariness', the narrator continually threatens to subvert or deconstruct the novelistic 'truth' of his tale. But then again, on resuming his narrative, he will recapture our interest in his heroes' fates and reignite an acceptance of their 'reality'. In his frequent address to both 'readers' and 'friends' (the latter comprised apparently of more sophisticated sorts of reader), the author anticipates almost all the potential ways of approaching and interpreting his book and seems to be trying to fashion, out of an amalgam of both naïve and sophisticated sensibilities, his ideal reader. We, his actual readers, like the solvers of a Chinese puzzle, must work out for ourselves the answers to a number of riddles the work proposes. What is the true nature of art? Where do the boundaries between literature and life lie? Or are there no boundaries, only a tangled network of intersecting threads that connect the lives we lead with the books we read? Perhaps, as this thoroughly modern and timeless work suggests, we are unable, despite all our strivings for personal 'authenticity', to be anything but the roles we play, the products and the playthings of literary and social conventions.

Pushkin's intricate and playful exploration of the connections between art and life permeates the work. His own practice as a poet is a case in point, issuing not only from his own genius, but from his enormous reading and his extensive knowledge of literary tradition. The novel's verse, poetry of the highest order, is also at times a pastiche of all the many clichés of poetic imagery and diction, of the techniques and formal conventions of a vast existing literature; though the writer may violate or mix or parody these traditions, he cannot exist without them. In support of its author's sly yet revealing game, the novel is full of literary allusions and references to other writers; it mocks the easy conflation of literature and life in countless ways: by the device, for example, of mixing real with fictional personages. Most prominently, of course, Pushkin has inserted himself into his book, not only as its narrator, but as the ostensible friend of its hero, Onegin. Tatyana, to give another instance, encounters and captivates at a Moscow soirée Prince Vyazemsky, Pushkin's actual friend and fellow-poet. When the poem momentarily turns historical novel, the Emperor Napoleon briefly appears, only to be condemned as the impostor (in Russian memory) whose heroic pretensions were consumed by a Moscow conflagration and by life's intractability. Napoleon also figures in the novel as an icon of the European romantic imagination and, ironically, as the idol of the westernized Russian Onegin, who keeps a statuette of his hero in his study.

Again and again the work demonstrates that cultural myths are deeply embedded in the modern consciousness, that we cannot disentangle ourselves from our words or extricate our 'selves' from our texts. None of this, happily, seems to make human nature in Pushkin's eyes any less real or human characters any less responsible for their actions. The disguises we wear and the poses we assume or, contrastingly, the more active and creative roles that we may elect to play in life, define us as human beings.

The early-nineteenth-century critic Belinsky remarked famously that Pushkin's novel is 'an encyclopedia of Russian life'. Although it is currently fashionable to disparage Belinsky's 'crudely sociological' approach to literature, there is much to be said (especially if we remove the word 'Russian') for his observation. For all this work's literary self-consciousness (it is an encyclopedia of literature, too), what a richly woven and glittering tapestry of life it contains, much of it supplied in apparently casual passing fashion, as was Pushkin's way. He shows us the theatre, where on a public stage writers, actors, and audience all perform and where the wings become a setting for erotic adventure; he gives us dance in its many shapes and styles: the ballet, the society ball, the country shindig, the peasant stomp; other music and song: in opera, in a regimental band, in the singing of serf-girls; food and dining, in fashionable restaurants and at rustic feasts; the architectural environment in churches, palaces, city mansions, apartments, urban hovels, and country manors; the varying styles of clothing; the books; the protocols of duelling; the customs of matchmaking, courtship, and marriage; life as played out in passionate youth and in resigned middle-age; the relationships of parents and children; the ways of the contemporary city and the ancient traditions of the countryside; the horses and conveyances that people use (which are also metaphors for the Pushkinian rush to experience life's variety, or at least to observe it from the window of a moving carriage)—all the activities, codes, customs, and conventions through which we live and which determine, whether we observe or defy them, who we are. And note as well the lively capsule biographies of some of the novel's minor characters: Tatyana's parents, Onegin's father and uncle, the rake Zaretsky, and even the two alternative futures imagined for Lensky beyond the novel's time-frame. Once again, in these mini-biographies, the author's touch is light and fleeting, his method the sparing use of a few trivial and prosaic details, the more insignificant the more telling.

Let me close these brief introductory remarks on Pushkin's masterwork with a few observations on some of its autobiographical implications. It presents, among its other texts, the writer's report to himself at mid-career, recording his discoveries about life and art and his concerns for his creative future. Not only the novel's narrator, it should be noted, but also the three other major characters are quite clearly expressions of Pushkin's personality. Onegin, despite the author's disclaimer to the contrary, bears some of Pushkin's own human traits, and the two share a number of social masks; the essential and decisive difference between them, of course, is that Onegin has none of the poet in him. Lensky, on the other hand, who does possess a genuine if immature poetic sensibility, is not unlike the younger Pushkin, a persona the writer has outgrown and now regards with affectionate irony. The conflict in the novel between Onegin and Lensky, so perplexingly motivated in terms of the characters' psychology, represents much more plausibly a conflict in the soul of the author, a struggle between his 'prosaic' and 'poetic' selves (recall the description when the two characters first meet: Lensky all poetry, Onegin all prose). If it seems that Pushkin takes the cynical Onegin rather seriously and merely mocks the naïve Lensky, this is something of a subterfuge, a device to conceal his own passionate commitment, even as he questions it, to poetry. Onegin, Pushkin's 'friend', is at once his baser *alter ego* and a symbol of his new allegiance to the truths of prose. Tatyana, whom the narrator calls his 'ideal' and who by the novel's end is identified with Pushkin's Muse, seems on a symbolic plane to stand as the artist's emblem for the native sources of his poetry, or as an avatar of his art itself. She is a figure who, though unhappy and unfree (like Pushkin himself), remains steadfast in her adherence to values beyond the gratifications of the self. There is an undeniable sadness in this sparkling novel, especially at its end. If it opened to the tune of a sprightly scherzo, it closes to the strains of a somewhat mournful adagio. Pain and disappointment have a prominent place in the world of *Onegin*, but so too does the celebration of life in all its enticing minutiae; and thus the novel gives us neither a conventionally happy nor a conventionally unhappy ending. It avoids, to be sure, any overt statement of tragedy, for the hero and heroine still live, are indeed still relatively young. Their stories, abruptly abandoned in typically Pushkinian fashion, remain incomplete, their ultimate fates still unresolved. In his final chapter does Pushkin even try to rescue his hapless hero from the shallowness of his egoism? Does he seek to make him worthy through his suffering of someone's, if not Tatyana's, love? Could the tale that unwinds beyond the pages of the book be resumed, could it take unexpected turns and move in new directions, are other outcomes possible? One suspects, despite the aesthetically pleasing roundedness of the poem, that the answers are *yes*, that other roads lie ahead for the heroes, that life still beckons. In his generosity of spirit the author gives to his characters, and thereby to himself, the possibility of renewal. The concluding chapters of *Eugene Onegin* are Pushkin's farewell to his poetic youth. Henceforth, in his effort to reinvent himself, and as a sign of his commitment to become yet more fully engaged in the life of literature, he would devote his energies mainly to prose. For Pushkin, however, to cease completely to be a poet was to die, and in his 'novel in verse' he announces a continuing will to live. Life's chalice, he tells us in its final stanza, never runs dry, life's novel (which the artist both reads and writes) never comes to an end for the taker of risks.

translator's quixotic quest, a quest in some respects not unlike that of the artist he seeks to emulate.

The other translators who have put Pushkin's novel into English have chosen, unlike Nabokov, to honour in most respects the 'Onegin stanza' and to retain the original's metrical scheme and rhyme. Two of them in particular, Walter Arndt and Charles Johnston, have done so with some success and have demonstrated thereby that the task may be slightly less impossible than it seems. My own attempt to pursue the elusive Pushkin yet again has profited much by their example, following them in their virtues and avoiding, as far as possible, their defects. If the results presented here are no less provisional than their efforts or the efforts of others that have gone before, I have none the less greatly enjoyed my pursuit of Pushkin and have found the view, even from the lower altitudes, well worth the climb.

I, too, have elected, in my version, to preserve what I could of Pushkin's form, taking the Onegin stanza as one of the novel's most essential and characteristic features, the building-block with which the entire edifice is constructed. By retaining the stanza form that Pushkin uses as his poetic paragraph, the translator positions himself, in a sense, on the work's home ground and imposes upon himself a useful discipline for his journey. Furthermore, he is thereby constrained, as was the poet himself, to seek solutions without self-indulgence, to find variety within oneness, and to earn freedom within the bondage of the form. The very rigidity of the stanzaic structure can bring at times a fruitful tension to the words with which the form is made manifest, and the economy of expression it enforces upon the translator will sometimes reward him with an unexpected gift.

In working, over quite a few years, on several visions and revisions of this translation, I have found myself searching for an ever more natural and unforced flow of language, for a more fluid and straightforward syntax, a lighter and more readily comprehensible style; I have tried to avoid as much as possible the sorts of inversions and verbal contortions that have marred in my view the earlier translations—all in an effort to capture what seemed to me the poem's spontaneous and unlaboured effect in Pushkin's Russian. I have also tried to adapt the rhythms of the poem to the rhythms of English speech—a speech that in my rendition sounds somewhat more American than British in its accent and somewhat more contemporary than period in its idiom. Ultimately, I have attempted to provide the English-speaking reader of today with a more accessible version of one of the great works of the Russian literary imagination, one that would speak in a familiar, not-too-distant English voice and that would convey not only something of the novel's sense and shape, but some hints of its characteristic flavour as well: its verve and sparkle, its lyricism and wit, its succinctness and variety: the play of lights and shadows in an imperfect mirror.

A few words on the Onegin stanza. The main body of the novel consists in its final form (some stanzas having been discarded by Pushkin for a variety of reasons) of some 366 stanzas of a common design. The fourteen lines of this stanzaic form suggest, of course, the sonnet, but the rhyming pattern is unique (ababccddeffegg), as is the adherence to a fixed sequence of masculine and feminine rhymes (that is, rhymes in which the stresses fall on the final or the penultimate syllables, respectively): FMFMFFMMFMMFMM. The metre, iambic tetrameter, though it may seem somewhat terse for a long narrative poem in English, is hardly in itself alien to our tradition. Compositionally, the stanzas are organized in a variety of ways: as a single unit, as octave and sestet, or as three quatrains and a couplet. The second quatrain may function as two couplets (ccdd), and the sestet as two linked tercets (eff egg). The three quatrains, it will be noted, employ in sequence the three possible patterns for a binary rhyme scheme: alternating (abab), balanced (ccdd), and enclosed (effe). Pushkin uses his sonnet-paragraph with great virtuosity and flexibility. The opening quatrain and the closing couplet are usually the most clearly marked, while the middle sections are treated with great variety. The final masculine couplet, especially, tends to stand out as a tersely pointed and often ironic coda.

There are considerably more than 5,000 lines of verse in this work, and the sheer quantity of its rhyme, it must be admitted, sorely tests the translator's inventiveness. I am also well aware that rhyme today is somewhat less common in serious English verse than it used to be and that its pervasiveness here may seem uncongenial to the modern ear. I rely, therefore, on the reader's tolerance for traditions beyond the borders of current taste and on the hope that something archaic may have grown so unfamiliar as to offer, perhaps, the pleasure of novelty. On some of the Russian names in the text and on a few other words I have placed an accent mark on the syllable that bears the stress; in general, however, the iambic metre should be a sufficient guide to the pronunciation of unfamiliar words. The Russian text used for this translation is essentially that used by Nabokov, the so-called 'third' edition, the last to be published during Pushkin's lifetime.

Finally, let me express once again my indebtedness to the previous translators of Pushkin's poem. Vladimir Nabokov's work, in particular, was a constant challenge to strive for greater accuracy, and his extensive commentary on the novel was an endless source of both instruction and pleasure. I want also to express my gratitude to Oxford University Press for giving me, in this second edition of my translation, the opportunity to revise the text and to add to it the verse fragments on 'Onegin's Journey' that Pushkin appended to his novel. I should like also to repeat my thanks to Professor Lauren Leighton of the University of Illinois at Chicago for his considerable support and encouragement and to my colleague John Osborne for patiently reading all those early drafts and for urging me, when my energy waned, to continue with a restless ingenuity. My wife, Eve, has been a sharp but always partial critic. To all those, including those unnamed, who have helped to improve this translation and to eliminate, at least in part, its lapses from sense and grace, many thanks.

SELECT BIBLIOGRAPHY

BARTA, P., and GOEBEL, U. (eds.), *The Contexts of Aleksandr Sergeevich Pushkin* (Lewiston, NY, 1988).

BAYLEY, J., *Pushkin: A Comparative Commentary* (Cambridge, 1971).

BETHEA, D. (ed.), *Pushkin Today* (Bloomington, Ind., 1993).

BLOOM, H., *Alexander Pushkin* (New York, 1987).

BRIGGS, A., *Alexander Pushkin: A Critical Study* (Totowa, NJ, 1983).

—— *Alexander Pushkin: Eugene Onegin* (Cambridge, 1992).

CHIZHEVSKY, D., *Evgenij Onegin* (Cambridge, Mass., 1953).

CLAYTON, J., *Ice and Flame: A. Pushkin's Eugene Onegin* (Toronto, 1985).

DEBRECZENY, P., *The Other Pushkin: A Study of Pushkin's Prose Fiction* (Stanford, Ca., 1983).

DRIVER, S., *Pushkin: Literature and Social Ideas* (New York, 1989).

FENNELL, J., *Pushkin* (Harmondsworth, 1964).

HOISINGTON, S., *Russian Views of Pushkin's 'Eugene Onegin'* (Bloomington, Ind., 1988).

JAKOBSON, R., *Pushkin and his Sculptural Myth*, tr. J. Burbank (The Hague, 1975).

KODJAK, A., and TARANOVSKY, K. (eds.), *Alexander Pushkin: A Symposium on the 175th Anniversary of his Birth* (New York, 1976).

—— —— *Alexander Pushkin Symposium II* (Columbus, Oh. 1980).

LAVRIN, J., *Pushkin and Russian Literature* (London, 1947).

LEVITT, M., *Russian Literary Politics and the Pushkin Celebration of 1880* (Ithaca, NY, 1989).

MAGARSHACK, D., *Pushkin: A Biography* (London, 1967).

MIRSKY, D., *Pushkin* (London, 1926; repr. New York, 1963).

NABOKOV, V., *Eugene Onegin: A Novel in Verse by Alexander Pushkin, Translated from the Russian with a Commentary*, 4 vols. (New York, 1964; rev. edn. Princeton, 1975).

PROFFER, C. (ed. and tr.), *The Critical Prose of Alexander Pushkin* (Bloomington, Ind. 1969).

RICHARDS, D., and COCKRELL, C. (eds.), *Russian Views of Pushkin* (Oxford, 1976).

SANDLER, S., *Distant Pleasures: Alexander Pushkin and the Writing of Exile* (Stanford, Ca., 1989).

SHAW, J. (ed.), *The Letters of Alexander Pushkin* (Bloomington, Ind. 1963).

—— *Pushkin's Rhymes* (Madison, Wis., 1974).

SHAW, J. *Pushkin: A Concordance to the Poetry* (Columbus, Oh., 1985).

SIMMONS, E., *Pushkin* (New York, 1964).

TERTZ, A. (Sinyavsky), *Strolls with Pushkin*, tr. C. Nepomnyashchy and S. Yastremski (New Haven, Conn., 1993).

TODD, W., *Fiction and Society in the Age of Pushkin* (Cambridge, Mass., 1986).

TROYAT, H., *Pushkin*, tr. N. Amphoux (London, 1974).

VICKERY, W., *Pushkin: Death of a Poet* (Bloomington, Ind., 1968).

——*Alexander Pushkin* (New York, 1970; rev. edn. New York, 1992).

WOLFF, T., *Pushkin on Literature* (London, 1971).

A CHRONOLOGY OF
ALEXANDER SERGEEVICH PUSHKIN

(all dates are old style)

1799   Born 26 May in Moscow. On his father's side Pushkin
was descended from a somewhat impoverished but
ancient aristocratic family. The poet's maternal great-
grandfather, Abram Hannibal, was an African princeling
(perhaps Abyssinian) who had been taken hostage as a
boy by the Turkish sultan. Brought eventually to Russia
and adopted by Peter the Great, he became a favourite
of the emperor and under subsequent rulers enjoyed a
distinguished career in the Russian military service. All
his life Pushkin retained great pride in his lineage on
both sides of the family.

1800–11   Entrusted in childhood to the care of governesses and
French tutors, Pushkin was largely ignored by his
parents. He did, however, avail himself of his father's
extensive library and read widely in French literature
of the seventeenth and eighteenth centuries. His
mastery of contemporary Russian speech owes much
to his early contact with household serfs, especially
with his nurse, Arina Rodionovna.

1811–17   Attends Lycée at Tsarskoe Selo near St Petersburg,
an academy newly established by Emperor Alexander
I for the education of young noblemen and their
preparation for government service. During these
school years he writes his earliest surviving verse.
Pushkin's poetic talent was recognized early and
admired by prominent Russian writers, including the
poets Derzhavin and Zhukovsky and the historian
Karamzin.

1817–20   Appointed to a sinecure in the Depártment of Foreign
Affairs, he leads a dissipated life in St Petersburg.

Writes satirical epigrams and circulates in manuscript form mildly seditious verse that incurs the displeasure of Emperor Alexander I. His first narrative poem, the mock epic *Ruslan and Lyudmila*, is published in 1820 and enjoys great success.

1820–4   Arrested for his liberal writings and exiled to service in the south of Russia (Ekaterinoslav, Kishinev, Odessa), he travels in the Caucasus, Crimea, Bessarabia. During this 'Byronic period' he composes his 'southern poems', including *The Prisoner of the Caucasus* and *The Fountain of Bakhchisarai*.

1823   Begins *Eugene Onegin* on 9 May (first chapter published in 1825).

1824   Writes narrative poem *The Gypsies*. After further conflict with the authorities he is dismissed from the service.

1824–6   Lives in exile for two more years at family estate of Mikhailovskoe.

1825   Writes verse drama *Boris Godunov*. Decembrist Revolt, in which several of the poet's friends participated, takes place while Pushkin is still absent from the capital.

1826–31   Pardoned by new Czar Nicholas I (September 1826) and allowed to return to Moscow, he resumes dissipated living. Continuing problems with censorship and growing dissatisfaction with the court and autocracy.

1827   Begins prose novel *The Moor of Peter the Great* (never completed), an account of the life and career of his ancestor Abram Hannibal.

1828   Writes narrative poem *Poltava* celebrating the victory of Peter the Great over Charles XII of Sweden.

1830   While stranded by a cholera epidemic at his country estate of Boldino he enjoys an especially productive autumn: effectively completes *Eugene Onegin*; writes *The Tales of Belkin* (prose stories); finishes 'Little

Tragedies': *The Covetous Knight*, *Mozart and Salieri*, *The Stone Guest*, *Feast in Time of Plague*.

1831   Marries Natalya Goncharova on 18 February; settles in St Petersburg; appointed official historiographer. Finally abandons work on *Eugene Onegin*, which has occupied him for more than eight years.

1831–7 Increasing personal and professional difficulties: financial troubles, unhappy married life, dismissal as a literary force by younger generation.

1833   Second 'Boldino autumn'. Writes short story *The Queen of Spades*, narrative poem *The Bronze Horseman*; works on *A History of the Pugachev Rebellion*

1836   Completes historical romance *The Captain's Daughter*.

1837   Incensed by the attentions paid to his wife by Baron Georges d'Antès, a French adventurer in the Russian service, Pushkin challenges him to a duel and on 27 February is mortally wounded; he dies two days later and his coffin is taken at night to Svyatogorsky Monastery near Mikhailovskoe for burial.

EUGENE ONEGIN

Pétri de vanité il avait encore plus
de cette espèce d'orgueil qui fait
avouer avec la même indifférence les
bonnes comme les mauvaises actions,
suite d'un sentiment de supériorité,
peut-être imaginaire.

Tiré d'une lettre particulière*

Dedication*

Not thinking of the proud world's pleasure,
But cherishing your friendship's claim,
I would have wished a finer treasure
To pledge my token to your name—
One worthy of your soul's perfection,
The sacred dreams that fill your gaze,
Your verse's limpid, live complexion,
Your noble thoughts and simple ways.
But let it be. Take this collection
Of sundry chapters as my suit:
Half humorous, half pessimistic,
Blending the plain and idealistic—
Amusement's yield, the careless fruit
Of sleepless nights, light inspirations,
Born of my green and withered years . . .
The intellect's cold observations,
The heart's reflections, writ in tears.

Chapter 1

To live he hurries and to feel makes haste.

Prince Vjazemsky

1

'My uncle, man of firm convictions* . . .
By falling gravely ill, he's won
A due respect for his afflictions—
The only clever thing he's done.
May his example profit others;
But God, what deadly boredom, brothers,
To tend a sick man night and day,
Not daring once to steal away!
And, oh, how base to pamper grossly
And entertain the nearly dead,
To fluff the pillows for his head,
And pass him medicines morosely—
While thinking under every sigh:
The devil take you, Uncle. Die!'

2

Just so a youthful rake reflected,
As through the dust by post he flew,
By mighty Zeus's will elected
Sole heir to all the kin he knew.
Ludmíla's and Ruslán's adherents!*
Without a foreword's interference,
May I present, as we set sail,
The hero of my current tale:
Onégin, my good friend and brother,
Was born beside the Neva's span,
Where maybe, reader, you began,
Or sparkled in one way or other.
I too there used to saunter forth,
But found it noxious in the north.*

3

An honest man who'd served sincerely,
His father ran up debts galore;
He gave a ball some three times yearly,
Until he had no means for more.
Fate watched Eugene in his dependence;
At first *Madame* was in attendance;
And then *Monsieur* took on the child,
A charming lad, though somewhat wild.
Monsieur l'Abbé, a needy fellow,
To spare his charge excessive pain,
Kept lessons light and rather plain;
His views on morals ever mellow,
He seldom punished any lark,
And walked the boy in Letny Park.*

4

But when the age of restless turnings
Became in time our young man's fate,
The age of hopes and tender yearnings,
Monsieur l'Abbé was shown the gate.
And here's Onegin—liberated,
To fad and fashion newly mated:
A London *dandy*, hair all curled,
At last he's ready for the world!
In French he could and did acutely
Express himself and even write;
In dancing too his step was light,
And bows he'd mastered absolutely.
Who'd ask for more? The world could tell
That he had wit and charm as well.

5

We've all received an education
In something somehow, have we not?
So thank the Lord that in this nation
A little learning means a lot.
Onegin was, so some decided
(Strict judges, not to be derided),
A learned, if pedantic, sort.
He did possess the happy forte
Of free and easy conversation,
Or in a grave dispute he'd wear
The solemn expert's learned air
And keep to silent meditation;
And how the ladies' eyes he lit
With flashes of his sudden wit!

6

The Latin vogue today is waning,
And yet I'll say on his behalf,
He had sufficient Latin training
To gloss a common epigraph,
Cite Juvenal in conversation,
Put *vale* in a salutation;
And he recalled, at least in part,
A line or two of Virgil's art.
He lacked, it's true, all predilection
For rooting in the ancient dust
Of history's annals full of must,
But knew by heart a fine collection
Of anecdotes of ages past:
From Romulus to Tuesday last.

7

Lacking the fervent dedication
That sees in sounds life's highest quest,
He never knew, to our frustration,
A dactyl from an anapest.
Theocritus and Homer bored him,
But reading Adam Smith restored him,
And economics he knew well;
Which is to say that he could tell
The ways in which a state progresses—
The actual things that make it thrive,
And why for gold it need not strive,
When *basic products* it possesses.
His father never understood
And mortgaged all the land he could.

8

I have no leisure for retailing
The sum of all our hero's parts,
But where his genius proved unfailing,
The thing he'd learned above all arts,
What from his prime had been his pleasure,
His only torment, toil, and treasure,
What occupied, the livelong day,
His languid spirit's fretful play
Was love itself, the art of ardour,
Which Ovid sang in ages past,
And for which song he paid at last
By ending his proud days a martyr—
In dim Moldavia's vacant waste,
Far from the Rome his heart embraced.

(9)* 10

How early on he could dissemble,
Conceal his hopes, play jealous swain,
Compel belief, or make her tremble,
Seem cast in gloom or mute with pain,
Appear so proud or so forbearing,
At times attentive, then uncaring!
What languor when his lips were sealed,
What fiery art his speech revealed!
What casual letters he would send her!
He lived, he breathed one single dream,
How self-oblivious he could seem!
How keen his glance, how bold and tender;
And when he wished, he'd make appear
The quickly summoned, glistening tear!

11

How shrewdly he could be inventive
And playfully astound the young,
Use flattery as warm incentive,
Or frighten with despairing tongue.
And how he'd seize a moment's weakness
To conquer youthful virtue's meekness
Through force of passion and of sense,
And then await sweet recompense.
At first he'd beg a declaration,
And listen for the heart's first beat,
Then stalk love faster—and entreat
A lover's secret assignation . . .
And then in private he'd prepare
In silence to instruct the fair!

12

How early he could stir or worry
The hearts of even skilled coquettes!
And when he found it necessary
To crush a rival—oh, what nets,
What clever traps he'd set before him!
And how his wicked tongue would gore him!
But you, you men in wedded bliss,
You stayed his friends despite all this:
The crafty husband fawned and chuckled
(Faublas'* disciple and his tool),
As did the skeptical old fool,
And the majestic, antlered cuckold—
So pleased with all he had in life:
Himself, his dinner, and his wife.

(13–14) 15

Some mornings still abed he drowses,
Until his valet brings his tray.
What? Invitations? Yes, three houses
Have asked him to a grand soirée.
There'll be a ball, a children's party;
Where will he dash to, my good hearty?
Where will he make the night's first call?
Oh, never mind—he'll make them all.
But meanwhile, dressed for morning pleasure,
Bedecked in broad-brimmed *Bolivár*,*
He drives to Nevsky Boulevard,
To stroll about at total leisure,
Until Bréguet's* unsleeping chime
Reminds him that it's dinner time.

16

He calls a sleigh as daylight's dimming;
The cry resounds: 'Make way! Let's go!'
His collar with its beaver trimming
Is silver bright with frosted snow.
He's off to Talon's,* late, and racing,
Quite sure he'll find Kavérin* pacing;
He enters—cork and bottle spout!
The comet wine* comes gushing out,
A bloody roastbeef's on the table,
And truffles, youth's delight so keen,
The very flower of French cuisine,
And Strasbourg pie,* that deathless fable;
While next to Limburg's lively mould
Sits ananás in splendid gold.

17

Another round would hardly hurt them,
To wash those sizzling cutlets down;
But now the chime and watch alert them:
The brand new ballet's on in town!
He's off!—this critic most exacting
Of all that touches art or acting,
This fickel swain of every star,
And honoured patron of the *barre*—
To join the crowd, where each is ready
To greet an *entrechat* with cheers,
Or Cleopatra with his jeers,
To hiss at Phèdre—so unsteady,
Recall Moïna* . . . and rejoice
That everyone has heard his voice.

18

Enchanted land! There for a season,
That friend of freedom ruled the scene,
The daring satirist Fonvízin,
As did derivative Knyazhnín;
There Ózerov received the nation's
Unbidden tears and its ovations,
Which young Semyónova did share;
And our Katénin gave us there
Corneille's full genius resurrected;
And there the caustic Shakhovskóy
Refreshed the stage with comic joy,
Didelot his crown of fame perfected.*
There too, beneath the theatre's tent,
My fleeting, youthful days were spent.

19

My goddesses! You vanished faces!
Oh, hearken to my woeful call:
Have other maidens gained your places,
Yet not replaced you after all?
Shall once again I hear your chants?
Or see the Russian muse of dance
Perform her soaring, soulful flight?
Or shall my mournful gaze alight
On unknown faces on the stages?
And when across this world I pass
A disenchanted opera glass,
Shall I grow bored with mirth and rages,
And shall I then in silence yawn
And recollect a time that's gone?

20

The theatre's full, the boxes glitter;
The restless gallery claps and roars;
The stalls and pit are all ajitter;
The curtain rustles as it soars.
And there . . . ethereal . . . resplendent,
Poised to the magic bow attendant,
A throng of nymphs her guardian band,
Istómina* takes up her stand.
One foot upon the ground she places,
And then the other slowly twirls,
And now she leaps! And now she whirls!
Like down from Eol's lips she races;
Then spins and twists and stops to beat
Her rapid, dazzling, dancing feet.

21

As all applaud, Onegin enters—
And treads on toes to reach his seat;
His double glass he calmly centres
On ladies he has yet to meet.
He takes a single glance to measure
These clothes and faces with displeasure;
Then trading bows on every side
With men he knew or friends he spied,
He turned at last and vaguely fluttered
His eyes toward the stage and play—
Then yawned and turned his head away:
'It's time for something new,' he muttered,
'I've suffered ballets long enough,
But now Didelot is boring stuff.'

22

While all those cupids, devils, serpents
Upon the stage still romp and roar,
And while the weary band of servants
Still sleeps on furs at carriage door;
And while the people still are tapping,
Still sniffling, coughing, hissing, clapping;
And while the lamps both in and out
Still glitter grandly all about;
And while the horses, bored at tether,
Still fidget, freezing, in the snow,
And coachmen by the fire's glow
Curse masters and beat palms together;
Onegin now has left the scene
And driven home to change and preen.

23

Shall I abandon every scruple
And picture truly with my pen
The room where fashion's model pupil
Is dressed, undressed, and dressed again?
Whatever clever London offers
To those with lavish whims and coffers,
And ships to us by Baltic seas
In trade for tallow and for trees;
Whatever Paris, seeking treasure,
Devises to attract the sight,
Or manufactures for delight,
For luxury, for modish pleasure—
All this adorned his dressing room,
Our sage of eighteen summers' bloom.

24

Imported pipes of Turkish amber,
Fine china, bronzes—all displayed;
And purely to delight and pamper,
Perfumes in crystal jars arrayed;
Steel files and combs in many guises,
Straight scissors, curved ones, thirty sizes
Of brushes for the modern male—
For hair and teeth and fingernail.
Rousseau (permit me this digression)
Could not conceive how solemn Grimm*
Dared clean his nails in front of *him*,
The brilliant madcap of confession.
In this case, though, one has to say
That Freedom's Champion went astray.

25

For one may be a man of reason
And mind the beauty of his nails.
Why argue vainly with the season?—
For custom's rule o'er man prevails.
Now my Eugene, Chadáyev's* double,
From jealous critics fearing trouble,
Was quite the pedant in his dress
And what we called a fop, no less.
At least three hours he peruses
His figure in the looking-glass;
Then through his dressing room he'll pass
Like flighty Venus when she chooses
In man's attire to pay a call
At masquerade or midnight ball.

26

Your interest piqued and doubtless growing
In current fashions of *toilette*,
I might describe in terms more knowing
His clothing for the learned set.
This might well seem an indiscretion,
Description, though, is my profession;
But *pantaloons, gilet,* and *frock—*
These words are hardly Russian stock;
And I confess (in public sorrow)
That as it is my diction groans
With far too many foreign loans;
But if indeed I overborrow,
I have of old relied upon
Our *Academic Lexicon.*

27

But let's abandon idle chatter
And hasten rather to forestall
Our hero's headlong, dashing clatter
In hired coach towards the ball.
Before the fronts of darkened houses,
Along a street that gently drowses,
The double carriage lamps in rows
Pour forth their warm and cheerful glows
And on the snow make rainbows glitter.
One splendid house is all alight,
Its countless lampions burning bright;
While past its glassed-in windows flitter
In quick succession silhouettes
Of ladies and their modish pets.

28

But look, Onegin's at the gateway;
He's past the porter, up the stair,
Through marble entry rushes straightway,
Then runs his fingers through his hair,
And steps inside. The crush increases,
The droning music never ceases;
A bold mazurka grips the crowd,
The press intense, the hubbub loud;
The guardsman clinks his spurs and dances,
The charming ladies twirl their feet—
Enchanting creatures that entreat
A hot pursuit of flaming glances;
While muffled by the violin
The wives their jealous gossip spin.

29

In days of dreams and dissipations
On balls I madly used to dote:
No surer place for declarations,
Or for the passing of a note.
And so I offer, worthy spouses,
My services to save your houses:
I pray you, heed my sound advice,
A word of warning should suffice.
You too, you mamas, I commend you
To keep your daughters well in sight;
Don't lower your lorgnettes at night!
Or else . . . or else . . . may God defend you!
All this I now can let you know,
Since I dropped sinning long ago.

30

So much of life have I neglected
In following where pleasure calls!
Yet were not morals ill affected
I even now would worship balls.
I love youth's wanton, fevered madness,
The crush, the glitter, and the gladness,
The ladies' gowns so well designed;
I love their feet—although you'll find
That all of Russia scarcely numbers
Three pairs of shapely feet . . . And yet,
How long it took me to forget
Two special feet. And in my slumbers
They still assail a soul grown cold
And on my heart retain their hold.

31

In what grim desert, madman, banished,
Will you at last cut memory's thread?
Ah, dearest feet, where have you vanished?
What vernal flowers do you tread?
Brought up in Oriental splendour,
You left no prints, no pressings tender,
Upon our mournful northern snow.
You loved instead to come and go
On yielding rugs in rich profusion;
While I—so long ago it seems!—
For your sake smothered all my dreams
Of glory, country, proud seclusion.
All gone are youth's bright years of grace,
As from the meadow your light trace.

32

Diana's breast is charming, brothers,
And Flora's cheek, I quite agree;
But I prefer above these others
The foot of sweet Terpsichore.
It hints to probing, ardent glances
Of rich rewards and peerless trances;
Its token beauty stokes the fires,
The wilful swarm of hot desires.
My dear Elvina, I adore it—
Beneath the table barely seen,
In springtime on the meadow's green,
In winter with the hearth before it,
Upon the ballroom's mirrored floor,
Or perched on granite by the shore.

33

I recollect the ocean rumbling:
O how I envied then the waves—
Those rushing tides in tumult tumbling
To fall about her feet like slaves!
I longed to join the waves in pressing
Upon those feet these lips . . . caressing.
No, never midst the fiercest blaze
Of wildest youth's most fervent days
Was I so racked with yearning's anguish:
No maiden's lips were equal bliss,
No rosy cheek that I might kiss,
Or sultry breast on which to languish.
No, never once did passion's flood
So rend my soul, so flame my blood.

34

Another memory finds me ready:
In cherished dreams I sometimes stand
And hold the lucky stirrup steady,
Then feel her foot within my hand!
Once more imagination surges,
Once more that touch ignites and urges
The blood within this withered heart:
Once more the love . . . once more the dart!
But stop . . . Enough! My babbling lyre
Has overpraised these haughty things:
They're hardly worth the songs one sings
Or all the passions they inspire;
Their charming words and glances sweet
Are quite as faithless as their feet.

35

But what of my Eugene? Half drowsing,
He drives to bed from last night's ball,
While Petersburg, already rousing,
Answers the drumbeat's duty call.
The merchant's up, the pedlar scurries,
With jug in hand the milkmaid hurries,
Crackling the freshly fallen snow;
The cabby plods to hackney row.
In pleasant hubbub morn's awaking!
The shutters open, smoke ascends
In pale blue shafts from chimney ends.
The German baker's up and baking,
And more than once, in cotton cap,
Has opened up his window-trap.

36

But wearied by the ballroom's clamour,
He sleeps in blissful, sheer delight—
This child of comfort and of glamour,
Who turns each morning into night.
By afternoon he'll finally waken,
The day ahead all planned and taken:
The endless round, the varied game;
Tomorrow too will be the same.
But was he happy in the flower—
The very springtime of his days,
Amid his pleasures and their blaze,
Amid his conquests of the hour?
Or was he profligate and hale
Amid his feasts to no avail?

37

Yes, soon he lost all warmth of feeling:
The social buzz became a bore,
And all those beauties, once appealing,
Were objects of his thought no more.
Inconstancy grew too fatiguing;
And friends and friendship less intriguing;
For after all he couldn't drain
An endless bottle of champagne
To help those pies and beefsteaks settle,
Or go on dropping words of wit
With throbbing head about to split:
And so, for all his fiery mettle,
He did at last give up his love
Of pistol, sword, and ready glove.

38

We still, alas, cannot forestall it—
This dreadful ailment's heavy toll;
The *spleen* is what the English call it,
We call it simply *Russian soul*.
'Twas this our hero had contracted;
And though, thank God, he never acted
To put a bullet through his head,
His former love of life was dead.
Like Byron's Harold, lost in trances,
Through drawing rooms he'd pass and stare;
But neither whist, nor gossip there,
Nor wanton sighs, nor tender glances—
No, nothing touched his sombre heart,
He noticed nothing, took no part.

(39–41) 42

Capricious belles of lofty station!
You were the first that he forswore;
For nowadays in our great nation,
The manner grand can only bore.
I wouldn't say that ladies never
Discuss a Say or Bentham*—ever;
But generally, you'll have to grant,
Their talk's absurd, if harmless, cant.
On top of which, they're so unerring,
So dignified, so awfully smart,
So pious and so chaste of heart,
So circumspect, so strict in bearing,
So inaccessibly serene,
Mere sight of them brings on the spleen.*

43

You too, young mistresses of leisure,
Who late at night are whisked away
In racing droshkies bound for pleasure
Along the Petersburg *chaussée*—
He dropped you too in sudden fashion.
Apostate from the storms of passion,
He locked himself within his den
And, with a yawn, took up his pen
And tried to write. But art's exaction
Of steady labour made him ill,
And nothing issued from his quill;
So thus he failed to join the faction
Of writers—whom I won't condemn
Since, after all, I'm one of them.

44

Once more an idler, now he smothers
The emptiness that plagues his soul
By making his the thoughts of others—
A laudable and worthy goal.
He crammed his bookshelf overflowing,
Then read and read—frustration growing:
Some raved or lied, and some were dense;
Some lacked all conscience; some, all sense;
Each with a different dogma girded;
The old was dated through and through,
While nothing new was in the new;
So books, like women, he deserted,
And over all that dusty crowd
He draped a linen mourning shroud.

45

I too had parted with convention,
With vain pursuit of worldly ends;
And when Eugene drew my attention,
I liked his ways and we made friends.
I liked his natural bent for dreaming,
His strangeness that was more than seeming,
The cold sharp mind that he possessed;
I was embittered, he depressed;
With passion's game we both were sated;
The fire in both our hearts was pale;
Our lives were weary, flat, and stale;
And for us both, ahead there waited—
While life was still but in its morn—
Blind fortune's malice and men's scorn.

46

He who has lived as thinking being
Within his soul must hold men small;
He who can feel is always fleeing
The ghost of days beyond recall;
For him enchantment's deep infection
Is gone; the snake of recollection
And grim repentance gnaws his heart.
All this, of course, can help impart
Great charm to private conversation;
And though the language of my friend
At first disturbed me, in the end
I liked his caustic disputation—
His blend of banter and of bile,
His sombre wit and biting style.

47

How often in the summer quarter,
When midnight sky is limpid–light
Above the Neva's placid water—
The river gay and sparkling bright,
Yet in its mirror not reflecting
Diana's visage—recollecting
The loves and intrigues of the past,
Alive once more and free at last,
We drank in silent contemplation
The balmy fragrance of the night!
Like convicts sent in dreaming flight
To forest green and liberation,
So we in fancy then were borne
Back to our springtime's golden morn.

48

Filled with his heart's regrets, and leaning
Against the rampart's granite shelf,
Eugene stood lost in pensive dreaming
(As once some poet drew himself*).
The night grew still . . . with silence falling;
Only the sound of sentries calling,
Or suddenly from Million Street
Some distant droshky's rumbling beat;
Or floating on the drowsy river,
A lonely boat would sail along,
While far away some rousing song
Or plaintive horn would make us shiver.
But sweeter still, amid such nights,
Are Tasso's octaves' soaring flights.

49

O Adriatic! Grand Creation!
O Brenta!* I shall yet rejoice,
When, filled once more with inspiration,
I hear at last your magic voice!
It's sacred to Apollo's choir;
Through Albion's great and haughty lyre*
It speaks to me in words I know.
On soft Italian nights I'll go
In search of pleasure's sweet profusion;
A fair Venetian at my side,
Now chatting, now a silent guide,
I'll float in gondola's seclusion;
And she my willing lips will teach
Both love's and Petrarch's ardent speech.

50

Will freedom come—and cut my tether?
It's time, it's time! I bid her hail;
I roam the shore,* await fair weather,
And beckon to each passing sail.
O when, my soul, with waves contesting,
And caped in storms, shall I go questing
Upon the crossroads of the sea?
It's time to quit this dreary lee
And land of harsh, forbidding places;
And there, where southern waves break high,
Beneath my Africa's warm sky,*
To sigh for sombre Russia's spaces,
Where first I loved, where first I wept,
And where my buried heart is kept.

51

Eugene and I had both decided
To make the foreign tour we'd planned;
But all too soon our paths divided,
For fate took matters into hand.
His father died—quite unexpected,
And round Eugene there soon collected
The greedy horde demanding pay.
Each to his own, or so they say.
Eugene, detesting litigation
And quite contented with his fate,
Released to them the whole estate . . .
With no great sense of deprivation;
Perhaps he also dimly knew
His aged uncle's time was due.

52

And sure enough a note came flying;
The bailiff wrote as if on cue:
Onegin's uncle, sick and dying,
Would like to bid his heir adieu.
He gave the message one quick reading,
And then by post Eugene was speeding,
Already bored, to uncle's bed,
While thoughts of money filled his head.
He was prepared—like any craven—
To sigh, deceive, and play his part
(With which my novel took its start);
But when he reached his uncle's haven,
A laid-out corpse was what he found,
Prepared as tribute for the ground.

53

He found the manor fairly bustling
With those who'd known the now deceased;
Both friends and foes had come ahustling,
True lovers of a funeral feast.
They laid to rest the dear departed;
Then, wined and dined and heavy-hearted,
But pleased to have their duty done,
The priests and guests left one by one.
And here's Onegin—lord and master
Of woods and mills and streams and lands;
A country squire, there he stands,
That former wastrel and disaster;
And rather glad he was, it's true,
That he'd found something else to do.

54

For two full days he was enchanted
By lonely fields and burbling brook,
By sylvan shade that lay implanted
Within a cool and leafy nook.
But by the third he couldn't stick it:
The grove, the hill, the field, the thicket—
Quite ceased to tempt him any more
And, presently, induced a snore;
And then he saw that country byways—
With no great palaces, no streets,
No cards, no balls, no poets' feats—
Were just as dull as city highways;
And spleen, he saw, would dog his life,
Like shadow or a faithful wife.

55

But I was born for peaceful roaming,
For country calm and lack of strife;
My lyre sings! And in the gloaming
My fertile fancies spring to life.
I give myself to harmless pleasures
And *far niente* rules my leisures:
Each morning early I'm awake
To wander by the lonely lake
Or seek some other sweet employment:
I read a little, often sleep,
For fleeting fame I do not weep.
And was it not in past enjoyment
Of shaded, idle times like this,
I spent my days of deepest bliss?

56

The country, love, green fields and flowers,
Sweet idleness! You have my heart.
With what delight I praise those hours
That set Eugene and me apart.
For otherwise some mocking reader
Or, God forbid, some wretched breeder
Of twisted slanders might combine
My hero's features here with mine
And then maintain the shameless fiction
That, like proud Byron, I have penned
A mere self-portrait in the end;
As if today, through some restriction,
We're now no longer fit to write
On any theme but our own plight.

57

All poets, I need hardly mention,
Have drawn from love abundant themes;
I too have gazed in rapt attention
When cherished beings filled my dreams.
My soul preserved their secret features;
The Muse then made them living creatures:
Just so in carefree song I paid
My tribute to the mountain maid,
And sang the Salghir captives' praises.*
And now, my friends, I hear once more
That question you have put before:
'For whom these sighs your lyre raises?
To whom amid the jealous throng
Do you today devote your song?

58

'Whose gaze, evoking inspiration,
Rewards you with a soft caress?
Whose form, in pensive adoration,
Do you now clothe in sacred dress?'
Why no one, friends, as God's my witness,
For I have known too well the witless
And maddened pangs of love's refrain.
Oh, blest is he who joins his pain
To fevered rhyme: for thus he doubles
The sacred ecstasy of art;
Like Petrarch then, he calms the heart,
Subduing passion's host of troubles,
And captures worldly fame to boot!—
But I, in love, was dense and mute.

59

The Muse appeared as love was ending
And cleared the darkened mind she found.
Once free, I seek again the blending
Of feeling, thought, and magic sound.
I write . . . and want no more embraces;
My straying pen no longer traces,
Beneath a verse left incomplete,
The shapes of ladies' heads and feet.
Extinguished ashes won't rekindle,
And though I grieve, I weep no more;
And soon, quite soon, the tempest's core
Within my soul will fade and dwindle:
And *then* I'll write this world a song
That's five and twenty cantos long!

60

I've drawn a plan and know what's needed,
The hero's named, the plotting's done;
And meantime I've just now completed
My present novel's Chapter One.
I've looked it over most severely;
It has its contradictions, clearly,
But I've no wish to change a line;
I'll grant the censor's right to shine
And send these fruits of inspiration
To feed the critics' hungry pen.
Fly to the Neva's water then,
My spirit's own newborn creation!
And earn me tribute paid to fame:
Distorted readings, noise, and blame!

Chapter 2

O rus!

      Horace

O Rus'!*

1

The place Eugene found so confining
Was quite a lovely country nest,
Where one who favoured soft reclining
Would thank his stars to be so blest.
The manor house, in proud seclusion,
Screened by a hill from wind's intrusion,
Stood by a river. Far away
Green meads and golden cornfields lay,
Lit by the sun as it paraded;
Small hamlets too the eye could see
And cattle wand'ring o'er the lea;
While near at hand, all dense and shaded,
A vast neglected garden made
A nook where pensive dryads played.

2

The ancient manse had been erected
For placid comfort—and to last;
And all its solid form reflected
The sense and taste of ages past.
Throughout the house the ceilings towered,
From walls ancestral portraits glowered;
The drawing room had rich brocades
And stoves of tile in many shades.
All this today seems antiquated—
I don't know why; but in the end
It hardly mattered to my friend,
For he'd become so fully jaded,
He yawned alike where'er he sat,
In ancient hall or modern flat.

3

He settled where the former squire
For forty years had heaved his sighs,
Had cursed the cook in useless ire,
Stared out the window, and squashed flies.
The furnishings were plain but stable:
A couch, two cupboards, and a table,
No spot of ink on oaken floors.
Onegin opened cupboard doors
And found in one a list of wages,
Some fruit liqueurs and applejack,
And in the next an almanac
From eighteen-eight with tattered pages;
The busy master never took
A glance in any other book.

4

Alone amid his new possessions,
And merely as an idle scheme,
Eugene devised a few concessions
And introduced a new regime.
A backwoods genius, he commuted
The old *corvée* and substituted
A quitrent at a modest rate;*
His peasants thanked their lucky fate,
But thrifty neighbours waxed indignant
And in their dens bewailed as one
The dreadful harm of what he'd done.
Still others sneered or turned malignant,
And everyone who chose to speak
Called him a menace and a freak.

5

At first the neighbours' calls were steady;
But when they learned that in the rear
Onegin kept his stallion ready
So he could quickly disappear
The moment one of them was sighted
Or heard approaching uninvited,
They took offence and, one and all,
They dropped him cold and ceased to call.
'The man's a boor, he's off his rocker.'
'Must be a Mason;* drinks, they say . . .
Red wine, by tumbler, night and day!'
'Won't kiss a lady's hand, the mocker.'
'Won't call me "sir" the way he should.'
The general verdict wasn't good.

6

Another squire chose this season
To reappear at his estate
And gave the neighbours equal reason
For scrutiny no less irate.
Vladímir Lénsky, just returning
From Göttingen with soulful yearning,
Was in his prime—a handsome youth
And poet filled with Kantian truth.
From misty Germany our squire
Had carried back the fruits of art:
A freedom-loving, noble heart,
A spirit strange but full of fire,
An always bold, impassioned speech,
And raven locks of shoulder reach.

7

As yet unmarked by disillusion
Or chill corruption's deadly grasp,
His soul still knew the warm effusion
Of maiden's touch and friendship's clasp.
A charming fool at love's vocation,
He fed on hope's eternal ration;
The world's fresh glitter and its call
Still held his youthful mind in thrall;
He entertained with fond illusions
The doubts that plagued his heart and will;
The goal of life, he found, was still
A tempting riddle of confusions;
He racked his brains and rather thought
That miracles could still be wrought.

8

He knew a kindred soul was fated
To join her life to his career,
That even now she pined and waited,
Expecting he would soon appear.
And he believed that men would tender
Their freedom for his honour's splendour;
That friendly hands would surely rise
To shatter slander's cup of lies;
That there exists a holy cluster
Of chosen ones whom men should heed,
A happy and immortal breed,
Whose potent light in all its lustre
Would one day shine upon our race
And grant the world redeeming grace.*

9

Compassion, noble indignation,
A perfect love of righteous ways,
And fame's delicious agitation
Had stirred his soul since early days.
He roamed the world with singing lyre
And found the source of lyric fire
Beneath the skies of distant lands,
From Goethe's and from Schiller's hands.
He never shamed, the happy creature,
The lofty Muses of his art;
He proudly sang with open heart
Sublime emotion's every feature,
The charm of gravely simple things,
And youthful hopes on youthful wings.

10

He sang of love, by love commanded,
A simple and affecting tune,
As clear as maiden thoughts, as candid
As infant slumber, as the moon
In heaven's peaceful desert flying,
That queen of secrets and of sighing.
He sang of parting and of pain,
Of something vague, of mists and rain;
He sang the rose, romantic flower,
And distant lands where once he'd shed
His living tears upon the bed
Of silence at a lonely hour;
He sang life's bloom gone pale and sere—
He'd almost reached his eighteenth year.

11

Throughout that barren, dim dominion
Eugene alone could see his worth;
And Lensky formed a low opinion
Of neighbours' feasts and rounds of mirth;
He fled their noisy congregations
And found their solemn conversations—
Of liquor, and of hay brought in,
Of kennels, and of distant kin,
Devoid of any spark of feeling
Or hint of inner lyric grace;
Both wit and brains were out of place,
As were the arts of social dealing;
But then their charming wives he found
At talk were even less profound.

12

Well-off . . . and handsome in addition,
Young Lensky seemed the perfect catch;
And so, by countryside tradition,
They asked him round and sought to match
Their daughters with this semi-Russian.
He'd call—and right away discussion
Would touch obliquely on the point
That bachelors' lives were out of joint;
And then the guest would be invited
To take some tea while Dunya poured;
They whisper: 'Dunya, don't look bored!'—
Then bring in her guitar, excited . . .
And then, good God, she starts to bawl:
'Come to my golden chamberhall!'

13

But Lensky, having no desire
For marriage bonds or wedding bell,
Had cordial hopes that he'd acquire
The chance to know Onegin well.
And so they met—like wave with mountain,
Like verse with prose, like flame with fountain:
Their natures distant and apart.
At first their differences of heart
Made meetings dull at one another's;
But then their friendship grew, and soon
They'd meet on horse each afternoon,
And in the end were close as brothers.
Thus people—so it seems to me—
Become good friends from sheer ennui.

14

But even friendships like our heroes'
Exist no more; for we've outgrown
All sentiments and deem men zeros—
Except of course ourselves alone.
We all take on Napoleon's features,
And millions of our fellow creatures
Are nothing more to us than tools . . .
Since feelings are for freaks and fools.
Eugene, of course, had keen perceptions
And on the whole despised mankind,
Yet wasn't, like so many, blind;
And since each rule permits exceptions,
He did respect a noble few,
And, cold himself, gave warmth its due.

15

He smiled at Lensky's conversation.
Indeed the poet's fervent speech,
His gaze of constant inspiration,
His mind, still vacillant in reach—
All these were new and unexpected,
And so, for once, Eugene elected
To keep his wicked tongue in check,
And thought: What foolishness to wreck
The young man's blissful, brief infection;
Its time will pass without my knife,
So let him meanwhile live his life
Believing in the world's perfection;
Let's grant to fevered youthful days
Their youthful ravings and their blaze.

16

The two found everything a basis
For argument or food for thought:
The covenants of bygone races,
The fruits that learned science brought,
The prejudice that haunts all history,
The grave's eternal, fateful mystery,
And Good and Evil, Life and Fate—
On each in turn they'd ruminate.
The poet, lost in hot contention,
Would oft recite, his eyes ablaze,
Brief passages from Nordic lays;
Eugene, with friendly condescension,
Would listen with a look intense,
Although he seldom saw their sense.

17

More often, though, my two recluses
Would muse on passions* and their flights.
Eugene, who'd fled their wild abuses,
Regretted still his past delights
And sighed, recalling their interment.
Oh, happy he who's known the ferment
Of passions and escaped their lot;
More happy he who knew them not,
Who cooled off love with separation
And enmity with harsh contempt;
Who yawned with wife and friends, exempt
From pangs of jealous agitation;
Who never risked his sound estate
Upon a deuce, that cunning bait.

18

When we at last turn into sages
And flock to tranquil wisdom's crest;
When passion's flame no longer rages,
And all the yearnings in our breast,
The wayward fits, the final surges,
Have all become mere comic urges,
And pain has made us humble men—
We sometimes like to listen then
As others tell of passions swelling;
They stir our hearts and fan the flame.
Just so a soldier, old and lame,
Forgotten in his wretched dwelling,
Will strain to hear with bated breath
The youngbloods' yarns of courting death.

19

But flaming youth in all its madness
Keeps nothing of its heart concealed:
Its loves and hates, its joy and sadness,
Are babbled out and soon revealed.
Onegin, who was widely taken
As one whom love had left forsaken,
Would listen gravely to the end
When self-expression gripped his friend;
The poet, feasting on confession,
Naïvely poured his secrets out;
And so Eugene learned all about
The course of youthful love's progression—
A story rich in feelings too,
Although to us they're hardly new.

20

Ah yes, he loved in such a fashion
As men today no longer do;
As only poets, mad with passion,
Still love . . . because they're fated to.
He knew one constant source of dreaming,
One constant wish forever gleaming,
One ever-present cause for pain!
And neither distance, nor the chain
Of endless years of separation,
Nor pleasure's rounds, nor learning's well,
Nor foreign beauties' magic spell,
Nor yet the Muse, his true vocation,
Could alter Lensky's deep desire,
His soul aflame with virgin fire.

21

When scarce a boy and not yet knowing
The torment of a heart in flames,
He'd been entranced by Olga growing
And fondly watched her girlhood games;
Beneath a shady park's protection
He'd shared her frolics with affection.
Their fathers, who were friends, had plans
To read one day their marriage banns.
And deep within her rustic bower,
Beneath her parents' loving gaze,
She blossomed in a maiden's ways—
A valley-lily come to flower
Off where the grass grows dense and high,
Unseen by bee or butterfly.

22

She gave the poet intimations
Of youthful ecstasies unknown,
And, filling all his meditations,
Drew forth his flute's first ardent moan.
Farewell, O golden games' illusion!
He fell in love with dark seclusion,
With stillness, stars, the lonely night,
And with the moon's celestial light—
That lamp to which we've consecrated
A thousand walks in evening's calm
And countless tears—the gentle balm
Of secret torments unabated . . . .
Today, though, all we see in her
Is just another lantern's blur.

23

Forever modest, meek in bearing,
As gay as morning's rosy dress,
Like any poet—open, caring,
As sweet as love's own soft caress;
Her sky-blue eyes, devoid of guile,
Her flaxen curls, her lovely smile,
Her voice, her form, her graceful stance,
Oh, Olga's every trait . . . . But glance
In any novel—you'll discover
Her portrait there; it's charming, true;
I liked it once no less than you,
But round it boredom seems to hover;
And so, dear reader, grant me pause
To plead her elder sister's cause.

24

Her sister bore the name Tatyana.
And we now press our wilful claim
To be the first who thus shall honour
A tender novel with that name.*
Why not? I like its intonation;
It has, I know, association
With olden days beyond recall,
With humble roots and servants' hall;
But we must grant, though it offend us:
Our taste in names is less than weak
(Of verses I won't even speak);
Enlightenment has failed to mend us,
And all we've learned from its great store
Is affectation—nothing more.

25

So she was called Tatyana, reader.
She lacked that fresh and rosy tone
That made her sister's beauty sweeter
And drew all eyes to her alone.
A wild creature, sad and pensive,
Shy as a doe and apprehensive,
Tatyana seemed among her kin
A stranger who had wandered in.
She never learned to show affection,
To hug her parents—either one;
A child herself, for children's fun
She lacked the slightest predilection,
And oftentimes she'd sit all day
In silence at the window bay.

26

But pensiveness, her friend and treasure
Through all her years since cradle days,
Adorned the course of rural leisure
By bringing dreams before her gaze.
She never touched a fragile finger
To thread a needle, wouldn't linger
Above a tambour to enrich
A linen cloth with silken stitch.
Mark how the world compels submission:
The little girl with docile doll
Prepares in play for protocol,
For every social admonition;
And to her doll, without demur,
Repeats what mama taught to her.

27

But dolls were never Tanya's passion,
When she was small she didn't choose
To talk to them of clothes or fashion
Or tell them all the city news.
And she was not the sort who glories
In girlish pranks; but grisly stories
Quite charmed her heart when they were told
On winter nights all dark and cold.
Whenever nanny brought together
Young Olga's friends to spend the day,
Tatyana never joined their play
Or games of tag upon the heather;
For she was bored by all their noise,
Their laughing shouts and giddy joys.

28

Upon her balcony appearing,
She loved to greet Aurora's show,
When dancing stars are disappearing
Against the heavens' pallid glow,
When earth's horizon softly blushes,
And wind, the morning's herald, rushes,
And slowly day begins its flight.
In winter, when the shade of night
Still longer half the globe encumbers,
And 'neath the misty moon on high
An idle stillness rules the sky,
And late the lazy East still slumbers—
Awakened early none the less,
By candlelight she'd rise and dress.

29

From early youth she read romances,
And novels set her heart aglow;
She loved the fictions and the fancies
Of Richardson and of Rousseau.
Her father was a kindly fellow—
Lost in a past he found more mellow;
But still, in books he saw no harm,
And, though immune to reading's charm,
Deemed it a minor peccadillo;
Nor did he care what secret tome
His daughter read or kept at home
Asleep till morn beneath her pillow;
His wife herself, we ought to add,
For Richardson was simply mad.

30

It wasn't that she'd read him, really,
Nor was it that she much preferred
To Lovelace Grandison, but merely
That long ago she'd often heard
Her Moscow cousin, Princess Laura,
Go on about their special aura.
Her husband at the time was still
Her fiancé—against her will!
For she, in spite of family feeling,
Had someone else for whom she pined—
A man whose heart and soul and mind
She found a great deal more appealing;
This Grandison was fashion's pet,
A gambler and a guards cadet.

31

About her clothes one couldn't fault her;
Like him, she dressed as taste decreed.
But then they led her to the altar
And never asked if she agreed.
The clever husband chose correctly
To take his grieving bride directly
To his estate, where first she cried
(With God knows whom on every side),
Then tossed about and seemed demented;
And almost even left her spouse;
But then she took to keeping house
And settled down and grew contented.
Thus heaven's gift to us is this:
That habit takes the place of bliss.

32

'Twas only habit then that taught her
The way to master rampant grief;
And soon a great discovery brought her
A final and complete relief.
Betwixt her chores and idle hours
She learned to use her woman's powers
To rule the house as autocrat,
And life went smoothly after that.
She'd drive around to check the workers,
She pickled mushrooms for the fall,
She made her weekly bathhouse call,
She kept the books, she shaved the shirkers,*
She beat the maids when she was cross—
And left her husband at a loss.

33

She used to write, with blood, quotations
In maidens' albums, thought it keen
To speak in singsong intonations,
Would call Praskóvya 'chère Pauline'.
She laced her corset very tightly,
Pronounced a Russian *n* as slightly
As *n* in French . . . and through the nose;
But soon she dropped her city pose:
The corset, albums, chic relations,
The sentimental verses too,
Were quite forgot; she bid adieu
To all her foreign affectations,
And took at last to coming down
In just her cap and quilted gown.

34

And yet her husband loved her dearly;
In all her schemes he'd never probe;
He trusted all she did sincerely
And ate and drank in just his robe.
His life flowed on—quite calm and pleasant—
With kindly neighbours sometimes present
For hearty talk at evenfall,
Just casual friends who'd often call
To shake their heads, to prate and prattle,
To laugh a bit at something new;
And time would pass, till Olga'd brew
Some tea to whet their tittle-tattle;
Then supper came, then time for bed,
And off the guests would drive, well fed.

35

Amid this peaceful life they cherished,
They held all ancient customs dear;
At Shrovetide feasts their table flourished
With Russian pancakes, Russian cheer;
Twice yearly too they did their fasting;
Were fond of songs for fortune-casting,
Of choral dances, garden swings.
At Trinity, when service brings
The people, yawning, in for prayer,
They'd shed a tender tear or two
Upon their buttercups of rue.
They needed *kvas* no less than air,
And at their table guests were served
By rank in turn as each deserved.*

36

And thus they aged, as do all mortals.
Until at last the husband found
That death had opened wide its portals,
Through which he entered, newly crowned.
He died at midday's break from labour,
Lamented much by friend and neighbour,
By children and by faithful wife—
Far more than some who part this life.
He was a kind and simple *barin*,
And there where now his ashes lie
A tombstone tells the passer-by:
The humble sinner Dmitry Larin
A slave of God and Brigadier
Beneath this stone now resteth here.

37

Restored to home and its safekeeping,
Young Lensky came to cast an eye
Upon his neighbour's place of sleeping,
And mourned his ashes with a sigh.
And long he stood in sorrow aching;
'Poor Yorick!' then he murmured, shaking,
'How oft within his arms I lay,
How oft in childhood days I'd play
With his Ochákov decoration!*
He destined Olga for my wife
And used to say: "Oh grant me, life,
To see the day!" ' . . . In lamentation,
Right then and there Vladimir penned
A funeral verse for his old friend.

38

And then with verse of quickened sadness
He honoured too, in tears and pain,
His parents' dust . . . their memory's gladness . . .
Alas! Upon life's furrowed plain—
A harvest brief, each generation,
By fate's mysterious dispensation,
Arises, ripens, and must fall;
Then others too must heed the call.
For thus our giddy race gains power:
It waxes, stirs, turns seething wave,
Then crowds its forebears toward the grave.
And we as well shall face that hour
When one fine day our grandsons true
Straight out of life will crowd us too!

39

So meanwhile, friends, enjoy your blessing:
This fragile life that hurries so!
Its worthlessness needs no professing,
And I'm not loathe to let it go;
I've closed my eyes to phantoms gleaming,
Yet distant hopes within me dreaming
Still stir my heart at times to flight:
I'd grieve to quit this world's dim light
And leave no trace, however slender.
I live, I write—not seeking fame;
And yet, I think, I'd wish to claim
For my sad lot its share of splendour—
At least one note to linger long,
Recalling, like some friend, my song.

40

And it may touch some heart with fire;
And thus preserved by fate's decree,
The stanza fashioned by my lyre
May yet not drown in Lethe's sea;
Perhaps (a flattering hope's illusion!)
Some future dunce with warm effusion
Will point my portrait out and plead:
'This was a poet, yes indeed!'
Accept my thanks and admiration,
You lover of the Muse's art,
O you whose mind shall know by heart
The fleeting works of my creation,
Whose cordial hand shall then be led
To pat the old man's laurelled head!

Chapter 3

Elle était fille, elle était
amoureuse.*

Malfilâtre

1

'Ah me, these poets . . . such a hurry!'
'Goodbye, Onegin . . . time I went.'
'Well, I won't keep you, have no worry,
But where are all your evenings spent?'
'The Larin place.'—'What reckless daring!
Good God, man, don't you find it wearing
Just killing time that way each night?'
'Why not at all.'—'Well, serves you right;
I've got the scene in mind so clearly:
For starters (tell me if I'm wrong),
A simple Russian family throng;
The guests all treated so sincerely;
With lots of jam and talk to spare.
On rain and flax and cattle care. . . .'

2

'Well, where's the harm . . . the evening passes.'
'The boredom, brother, there's the harm.'
'Well, I despise your upper classes
And *like* the family circle's charm;
It's where I find . . .'—'More pastoral singing!
Enough, old boy, my ears are ringing!
And so you're off . . . forgive me then.
But tell me Lensky, how and when
I'll see this Phyllis so provoking—
Who haunts your thoughts and writer's quill,
Your tears and rhymes and what-you-will?
Present me, do.'—'You must be joking!'
'I'm not.'—'Well then, why not tonight?
They'll welcome us with great delight.'

3

'Let's go.'
              And so the friends departed—
And on arrival duly meet
That sometimes heavy, but good-hearted,
Old-fashioned Russian welcome treat.
The social ritual never changes:
The hostess artfully arranges
On little dishes her preserves,
And on her covered table serves
A drink of lingonberry flavour.
With folded arms, along the hall,
The maids have gathered, one and all,
To glimpse the Larins' brand new neighbour;
While in the yard their men reproach
Onegin's taste in horse and coach.*

4

Now home's our heroes' destination,
As down the shortest road they fly;
Let's listen to their conversation
And use a furtive ear to spy.
'Why all these yawns, Onegin? Really!'
'Mere habit, Lensky.'—'But you're clearly
More bored than usual.'—'No, the same.
The fields are dark now, what a shame.
Come on, Andryúshka, faster, matey!
These stupid woods and fields and streams!
Oh, by the way, Dame Larin seems
A simple but a nice old lady;
I fear that lingonberry brew
May do me in before it's through.'

5

'But tell me, which one was Tatyana?'
'Why, she who with a wistful air—
All sad and silent like Svetlana*—
Came in and took the window chair.'
'And really you prefer the other?'
'Why not?'—'Were I the poet, brother,
I'd choose the elder one instead—
Your Olga's look is cold and dead,
As in some dull, Van Dyck madonna;
So round and fair of face is she,
She's like that stupid moon you see,
Up in that stupid sky you honour.'
Vladimir gave a curt reply
And let the conversation die.

6

Meanwhile . . . Onegin's presentation
At Madame Larin's country seat
Produced at large a great sensation
And gave the neighbours quite a treat.
They all began to gossip slyly,
To joke and comment (rather wryly);
And soon the general verdict ran,
That Tanya'd finally found a man;
Some even knowingly conceded
That wedding plans had long been set,
And then postponed till they could get
The stylish rings the couple needed.
As far as Lensky's wedding stood,
They knew they'd settled *that* for good.

7

Tatyana listened with vexation
To all this gossip; but it's true
That with a secret exultation,
Despite herself she wondered too;
And in her heart the thought was planted . . .
Until at last her fate was granted:
She fell in love. For thus indeed
Does spring awake the buried seed.
Long since her keen imagination,
With tenderness and pain imbued,
Had hungered for the fatal food;
Long since her heart's sweet agitation
Had choked her maiden breast too much:
Her soul awaited . . . someone's touch.

8

And now at last the wait has ended;
Her eyes have opened . . . seen his face!
And now, alas! . . . she lives attended—
All day, all night, in sleep's embrace—
By dreams of him; each passing hour
The world itself with magic power
But speaks of him. She cannot bear
The way the watchful servants stare,
Or stand the sound of friendly chatter.
Immersed in gloom beyond recall,
She pays no heed to guests at all,
And damns their idle ways and patter,
Their tendency to just drop in—
And talk all day once they begin.

9

And now with what great concentration
To tender novels she retreats,
With what a vivid fascination
Takes in their ravishing deceits!
Those figures fancy has created
Her happy dreams have animated:
The lover of Julíe Wolmár,*
Malék-Adhél* and de Linár,*
And Werther, that rebellious martyr,
And Grandison, the noble lord
(With whom today we're rather bored)—
All these our dreamy maiden's ardour
Has pictured with a single grace,
And seen in all . . . Onegin's face.

10

And then her warm imagination
Perceives herself as *heroine*—
Some favourite author's fond creation:
Clarissa,* Julia,* or Delphine.*
She wanders with her borrowed lovers
Through silent woods and so discovers
Within a book her heart's extremes,
Her secret passions, and her dreams.
She sighs . . . and in her soul possessing
Another's joy, another's pain,
She whispers in a soft refrain
The letter she would send caressing
Her hero . . . who was none the less
No Grandison in Russian dress.

11

Time was, with grave and measured diction,
A fervent author used to show
The hero in his work of fiction
Endowed with bright perfection's glow.
He'd furnish his beloved child—
Forever hounded and reviled—
With tender soul and manly grace,
Intelligence and handsome face.
And nursing noble passion's rages,
The ever dauntless hero stood
Prepared to die for love of good;
And in the novel's final pages,
Deceitful vice was made to pay
And honest virtue won the day.

12

But now our minds have grown inactive,
We're put to sleep by talk of 'sin';
Our novels too make vice attractive,
And even there it seems to win.
It's now the British Muse's fables
That lie on maidens' bedside tables
And haunt their dreams. They worship now
The Vampire with his pensive brow,
Or gloomy Melmoth, lost and pleading,
The Corsair, or the Wandering Jew,
And enigmatic Sbogar* too.
Lord Byron, his caprice succeeding,
Cloaked even hopeless egotism
In saturnine romanticism.

13

But what's the point? I'd like to know it.
Perhaps, my friends, by fate's decree,
I'll cease one day to be a poet—
When some new demon seizes me;
And scorning then Apollo's ire
To humble prose I'll bend my lyre:
A novel in the older vein
Will claim what happy days remain.
No secret crimes or passions gory
Shall I in grim detail portray,
But simply tell as best I may
A Russian family's age-old story,
A tale of lovers and their lot,
Of ancient customs unforgot.

14

I'll give a father's simple greetings,
An aged uncle's—in my book;
I'll show the children's secret meetings
By ancient lindens near the brook,
Their jealous torments, separation,
Their tears of reconciliation;
I'll make them quarrel yet again,
But lead them to the altar then.
I'll think up speeches tenderhearted,
Recall the words of passion's heat,
Those words with which—before the feet
Of some fair mistress long departed—
My heart and tongue once used to soar,
But which today I use no more.

15

Tatyana, O my dear Tatyana!
I shed with you sweet tears too late;
Relying on a tyrant's honour,
You've now resigned to him your fate.
My dear one, you are doomed to perish;
But first in dazzling hope you nourish
And summon forth a sombre bliss,
You learn life's sweetness . . . feel its kiss,
And drink the draught of love's temptations,
As phantom daydreams haunt your mind:
On every side you seem to find
Retreats for happy assignations;
While everywhere before your eyes
Your fateful tempter's figure lies.

16

The ache of love pursues Tatyana;
She takes a garden path and sighs,
A sudden faintness comes upon her,
She can't go on, she shuts her eyes;
Her bosom heaves, her cheeks are burning,
Scarce-breathing lips grow still with yearning,
Her ears resound with ringing cries,
And sparkles dance before her eyes.
Night falls; the moon begins parading
The distant vault of heaven's hood;
The nightingale in darkest wood
Breaks out in mournful serenading.
Tatyana tosses through the night
And wakes her nurse to share her plight.

17

'I couldn't sleep . . . O nurse, it's stifling!
Put up the window . . . sit by me.'
'What ails you, Tanya?'—'Life's so trifling,
Come tell me how it used to be.'
'Well, what about it? Lord, it's ages . . .
I must have known a thousand pages
Of ancient facts and fables too
'Bout evil ghosts and girls like you;
But nowadays I'm not so canny,
I can't remember much of late.
Oh, Tanya, it's a sorry state;
I get confused . . .' — 'But tell me, nanny,
About the olden days . . . you know,
Were you in love then, long ago?'

18

'Oh, come! Our world was quite another!
We'd never heard of love, you see.
Why, my good husband's sainted mother
Would just have been the death of me!'
'Then how'd you come to marry, nanny?'
'The will of God, I guess . . . . My Danny
Was younger still than me, my dear,
And I was just thirteen that year.
The marriage maker kept on calling
For two whole weeks to see my kin,
Till father blessed me and gave in.
I got so scared . . . my tears kept falling;
And weeping, they undid my plait,
Then sang me to the churchyard gate.

19

'And so they took me off to strangers . . .
But you're not even listening, pet.'
'Oh, nanny, life's so full of dangers,
I'm sick at heart and all upset,
I'm on the verge of tears and wailing!'
'My goodness, girl, you must be ailing;
Dear Lord have mercy. God, I plead!
Just tell me, dearest, what you need.
I'll sprinkle you with holy water,
You're burning up!'—'Oh, do be still,
I'm . . . you know, nurse . . . in love, not ill.'
'The Lord be with you now, my daughter!'
And with her wrinkled hand the nurse
Then crossed the girl and mumbled verse.

20

'Oh, I'm in love,' again she pleaded
With her old friend. 'My little dove,
You're just not well, you're overheated.'
'Oh, let me be now . . . I'm in love.'
And all the while the moon was shining
And with its murky light defining
Tatyana's charms and pallid air,
Her long, unloosened braids of hair,
And drops of tears . . . while on a hassock,
Beside the tender maiden's bed,
A kerchief on her grizzled head,
Sat nanny in her quilted cassock;
And all the world in silence lay
Beneath the moon's seductive ray.

21

Far off Tatyana ranged in dreaming,
Bewitched by moonlight's magic curse. . .
And then a sudden thought came gleaming:
'I'd be alone now . . . leave me, nurse.
But give me first a pen and paper;
I won't be long . . . just leave the taper.
Good night.' She's now alone. All's still.
The moonlight shines upon her sill.
And propped upon an elbow, writing,
Tatyana pictures her Eugene,
And in a letter, rash and green,
Pours forth a maiden's blameless plighting.
The letter's ready—all but sent. . .
For whom, Tatyana, is it meant?

22

I've known great beauties proudly distant,
As cold and chaste as winter snow;
Implacable, to all resistant,
Impossible for mind to know;
I've marvelled at their haughty manner,
Their natural virtue's flaunted banner;
And I confess, from them I fled,
As if in terror I had read
Above their brows the sign of Hades:
Abandon Hope, Who Enter Here!
Their joy is striking men with fear,
For love offends these charming ladies.
Perhaps along the Neva's shore
You too have known such belles before.

23

Why I've seen ladies so complacent
Before their loyal subjects' gaze,
That they would even grow impatient
With sighs of passion and with praise.
But what did I, amazed, discover?
On scaring off some timid lover
With stern behaviour's grim attack,
These creatures then would lure him back!—
By joining him at least in grieving,
By seeming in their words at least
More tender to the wounded beast;
And blind as ever, still believing,
The youthful lover with his yen
Would chase sweet vanity again.

24

So why is Tanya, then, more tainted?
Is it because her simple heart
Believes the chosen dream she's painted
And in deceit will take no part?
Because she heeds the call of passion
In such an honest, artless fashion?
Because she's trusting more than proud,
And by the Heavens was endowed
With such a rashness in surrender,
With such a lively mind and will,
And with a spirit never still,
And with a heart that's warm and tender?
But can't you, friends, forgive her, pray,
The giddiness of passion's sway?

25

'

The flirt will always reason coldly;
Tatyana's love is deep and true:
She yields without conditions, boldly—
As sweet and trusting children do.
She does not say: 'Let's wait till later
To make love's value all the greater
And bind him tighter with our rope;
Let's prick vainglory first with hope,
And then with doubt in fullest measure
We'll whip his heart, and when it's tame . . .
Revive it with a jealous flame;
For otherwise, grown bored with pleasure,
The cunning captive any day
Might break his chains and slip away.'

26

I face another complication:
My country's honour will demand
Without a doubt a full translation
Of Tanya's letter from my hand.
She knew the Russian language badly,
Ignored our journals all too gladly,
And in her native tongue, I fear,
Could barely make her meaning clear;
And so she turned for love's discussion
To French. . . . There's nothing I can do!
A lady's love, I say to you,
Has never been expressed in Russian;
Our mighty tongue, God only knows,
Has still not mastered postal prose.

27

Some would that ladies be required
To read in Russian. Dread command!
Why, I can picture them—inspired,
*The Good Samaritan** in hand!
I ask you now to tell me truly,
You poets who have sinned unduly:
Have not those creatures you adore,
Those objects of your verse . . . and more,
Been weak at Russian conversation?
And have they not, the charming fools,
Distorted sweetly all the rules
Of usage and pronunciation;
While yet a foreign language slips
With native glibness from their lips?

28

God spare me from the apparition,
On leaving some delightful ball,
Of bonneted Academician
Or scholar in a yellow shawl!
I find a faultless Russian style
Like crimson lips without a smile,
Mistakes in grammar charm the mind.
Perhaps (if fate should prove unkind!)
This generation's younger beauties,
Responding to our journals' call,
With grammar may delight us all,
And verses will be common duties.
But what care I for all they do?
To former ways I'll still be true.

29

A careless drawl, a tiny stutter,
Some imprecision of the tongue—
Can still produce a lovely flutter
Within this breast no longer young;
I lack the strength for true repentance,
And Gallicisms in a sentence
Seem sweet as youthful sins remote,
Or verse that Bogdanóvich* wrote.
But that will do. My beauty's letter
Must occupy my pen for now;
I gave my word, but, Lord, I vow,
Retracting it would suit me better.
I know that gentle Parny's* lays
Are out of fashion nowadays.

30

Bard of *The Feasts** and languid sorrow,
If you were with me still, my friend,
Immodestly I'd seek to borrow
Your genius for a worthy end:
I'd have you with your art refashion
A maiden's foreign words of passion
And make them magic songs anew.
Where are you? Come! I bow to you
And yield my rights to love's translation. . . .
But there beneath the Finnish sky,
Amid those mournful crags on high,
His heart grown deaf to commendation—
Alone upon his way he goes
And does not heed my present woes.

31

Tatyana's letter lies beside me,
And reverently I guard it still;
I read it with an ache inside me
And cannot ever read my fill.
Who taught her then this soft surrender,
This careless gift for waxing tender,
This touching whimsy free of art,
This raving discourse of the heart—
Enchanting, yet so fraught with trouble?
I'll never know. But none the less,
I give it here in feeble dress:
A living picture's pallid double,
Or *Freischütz** played with timid skill
By fingers that are learning still.

Tatyana's Letter to Onegin

I'm writing you this declaration—
What more can I in candour say?
It may be now your inclination
To scorn me and to turn away;
But if my hapless situation
Evokes some pity for my woe,
You won't abandon me, I know.
I first tried silence and evasion;
Believe me, you'd have never learned
My secret shame, had I discerned
The slightest hope that on occasion—
But once a week—I'd see your face,
Behold you at our country place,
Might hear you speak a friendly greeting,
Could say a word to you; and then,
Could dream both day and night again
Of but one thing, till our next meeting.

They say you like to be alone
And find the country unappealing;
We lack, I know, a worldly tone,
But still, we welcome you with feeling.

Why did you ever come to call?
In this forgotten country dwelling
I'd not have known you then at all,
Nor known this bitter heartache's swelling.
Perhaps, when time had helped in quelling
The girlish hopes on which I fed,
I might have found (who knows?) another
And been a faithful wife and mother,
Contented with the life I led.

Another! No! In all creation
There's no one else whom I'd adore;
The heavens chose my destination
And made me thine for evermore!
My life till now has been a token
In pledge of meeting you, my friend;
And in your coming, God has spoken,
You'll be my guardian till the end....

You filled my dreams and sweetest trances;
As yet unseen, and yet so dear,
You stirred me with your wondrous glances,
Your voice within my soul rang clear....
And then the dream came true for me!
When you came in, I seemed to waken,
I turned to flame, I felt all shaken,
And in my heart I cried: It's he!

And was it you I heard replying
Amid the stillness of the night,
Or when I helped the poor and dying,
Or turned to heaven, softly crying,
And said a prayer to soothe my plight?
And even now, my dearest vision,
Did I not see your apparition
Flit softly through this lucent night?
Was it not you who seemed to hover
Above my bed, a gentle lover,
To whisper hope and sweet delight?

Are you my angel of salvation
Or hell's own demon of temptation?

Be kind and send my doubts away;
For this may all be mere illusion,
The things a simple girl would say,
While Fate intends no grand conclusion. . . .

So be it then! Henceforth I place
My faith in you and your affection;
I plead with tears upon my face
And beg you for your kind protection.
You cannot know: I'm so alone,
There's no one here to whom I've spoken,
My mind and will are almost broken,
And I must die without a moan.
I wait for you . . . and your decision:
Revive my hopes with but a sign,
Or halt this heavy dream of mine—
Alas, with well-deserved derision!

I close. I dare not now reread. . . .
I shrink with shame and fear. But surely,
Your honour's all the pledge I need,
And I submit to it securely.

32

The letter trembles in her fingers;
By turns Tatyana groans and sighs.
The rosy sealing wafer lingers
Upon her fevered tongue and dries.
Her head is bowed, as if she's dozing;
Her light chemise has slipped, exposing
Her lovely shoulder to the night.
But now the moonbeams' glowing light
Begins to fade. The vale emerges
Above the mist. And now the stream
In silver curves begins to gleam.
The shepherd's pipe resounds and urges
The villager to rise. It's morn!
My Tanya, though, is so forlorn.

33

She takes no note of dawn's procession,
Just sits with lowered head, remote;
Nor does she put her seal's impression
Upon the letter that she wrote.
But now her door is softly swinging:
It's grey Filátievna, who's bringing
Her morning tea upon a tray.
'It's time, my sweet, to greet the day;
Why, pretty one, you're up already!
You're still my little early bird!
Last night you scared me, 'pon my word!
But thank the Lord, you seem more steady;
No trace at all of last night's fret,
Your cheeks are poppies now, my pet.'

34

'Oh, nurse, a favour, please . . . and hurry!'
'Why, sweetheart, anything you choose.'
'You mustn't think . . . and please don't worry . . .
But see . . . Oh, nanny, don't refuse!'
'As God's my witness, dear, I promise.'
'Then send your grandson, little Thomas,
To take this note of mine to O——,
Our neighbour, nurse, the one. . . you know!
And tell him that he's not to mention
My name, or breathe a single word. . . .'
'But who's it for, my little bird?
I'm trying hard to pay attention;
But we have lots of neighbours call,
I couldn't even count them all.'

35

'Oh nurse, your wits are all befuddled!'
'But, sweetheart, I've grown old . . . I mean . . .
I'm old; my mind . . . it does get muddled.
There was a time when I was keen,
When just the master's least suggestion. . . .'
'Oh, nanny, please, that's not the question,
It's not your mind I'm talking of,
I'm thinking of Onegin, love;
This note's to him.'—'Now don't get riled,
You know these days I'm not so clear,
I'll take the letter, never fear.
But you've gone pale again, my child!'
'It's nothing, nanny, be at ease,
Just send your grandson, will you please.'

36

The day wore on, no word came flying.
Another fruitless day went by.
All dressed since dawn, dead-pale and sighing,
Tatyana waits: will he reply?
Then Olga's suitor came a-wooing.
'But tell me, what's your friend been doing?'
Asked Tanya's mother, full of cheer;
'He's quite forgotten us, I fear.'
Tatyana blushed and trembled gently.
'He promised he would come today,'
Said Lensky in his friendly way,
'The mail has kept him evidently.'
Tatyana bowed her head in shame,
As if they all thought her to blame.

37

'Twas dusk; and on the table, gleaming,
The evening samovar grew hot;
It hissed and sent its vapour steaming
In swirls about the china pot.
And soon the fragrant tea was flowing
As Olga poured it, dark and glowing,
In all the cups; without a sound
A serving boy took cream around.
Tatyana by the window lingers
And breathes upon the chilly glass;
All lost in thought, the gentle lass
Begins to trace with lovely fingers
Across the misted panes a row
Of hallowed letters: *E* and *O*.

38

And all the while her soul was aching,
Her brimming eyes could hardly see.
Then sudden hoofbeats! . . . Now she's quaking. . . .
They're closer . . . coming here . . . it's he!
Onegin! 'Oh!'—And light as air,
She's out the backway, down the stair
From porch to yard, to garden straight;
She runs, she flies; she dare not wait
To glance behind her; on she pushes—
Past garden plots, small bridges, lawn,
The lakeway path, the wood; and on
She flies and breaks through lilac bushes,
Past seedbeds to the brook—so fast
That, panting, on a bench at last

39

She falls . . . .
       'He's here! But all those faces!
O God, what must he think of me!'
But still her anguished heart embraces
A misty dream of what might be.
She trembles, burns, and waits . . . so near him!
But will he come? . . . She doesn't hear him.
Some serf girls in the orchard there,
While picking berries, filled the air
With choral song—as they'd been bidden
(An edict that was meant, you see,
To keep sly mouths from feeling free
To eat the master's fruit when hidden,
By filling them with song instead—
For rural cunning isn't dead!):

The Girls' Song

'Lovely maidens, pretty ones,
Dearest hearts and darling friends,
Romp away, sweet lassies, now,
Have your fling, my dear ones, do!
Strike you up a rousing song,
Sing our secret ditty now,
Lure some likely lusty lad
To the circle of our dance.

When we lure the fellow on,
When we see him from afar,
Darlings, then, let's scamper off,
Pelting him with cherries then,
Cherries, yes, and raspberries,
Ripe red currants let us throw!

Never come to listen in
When we sing our secret songs,
Never come to spy on us
When we play our maiden games!'

40

Tatyana listens, scarcely hearing
The vibrant voices, sits apart,
And waits impatient in her clearing
To calm the tremor in her heart
And halt the constant surge of blushes;
But still her heart in panic rushes,
Her cheeks retain their blazing glow
And ever brighter, brighter grow.
Just so a butterfly both quivers
And beats an iridescent wing
When captured by some boy in spring;
Just so a hare in winter shivers,
When suddenly far off it sees
The hunter hiding in the trees.

41

But finally she rose, forsaken,
And, sighing, started home for bed;
But hardly had she turned and taken
The garden lane, when straight ahead,
His eyes ablaze, Eugene stood waiting—
Like some grim shade of night's creating;
And she, as if by fire seared,
Drew back and stopped when he appeared. . . .
Just now though, friends, I feel too tired
To tell you how this meeting went
And what ensued from that event;
I've talked so long that I've required
A little walk, some rest and play;
I'll finish up another day.

Chapter 4

La morale est dans la nature des choses*

Necker

(1–6) 7

The less we love her when we woo her,
The more we draw a woman in,
And thus more surely we undo her
Within the witching webs we spin.
Time was, when cold debauch was lauded
As love's high art . . . and was applauded
For trumpeting its happy lot
In taking joy while loving not.
But that pretentious game is dated,
But fit for apes, who once held sway
Amid our forbears' vaunted day;
The fame of Lovelaces has faded—
Along with fashions long since dead:
Majestic wigs and heels of red.

8

Who doesn't find dissembling dreary;
Or trying gravely to convince
(Recasting platitudes till weary)—
When all agree and have long since;
How dull to hear the same objections,
To overcome those predilections
That no young girl thirteen, I vow,
Has ever had and hasn't now!
Who wouldn't grow fatigued with rages,
Entreaties, vows, pretended fears,
Betrayals, gossip, rings, and tears,
With notes that run to seven pages,
With watchful mothers, aunts who stare,
And friendly husbands hard to bear!

9

Well, this was my Eugene's conclusion.
In early youth he'd been the prey
Of every raging mad delusion,
And uncurbed passions ruled the day.
Quite pampered by a life of leisure,
Enchanted with each passing pleasure,
But disenchanted just as quick,
Of all desire at length grown sick,
And irked by fleet success soon after,
He'd hear mid hum and hush alike
His grumbling soul the hours strike,
And smothered yawns with brittle laughter:
And so he killed eight years of youth
And lost life's very bloom, in truth.

10

He ceased to know infatuation,
Pursuing belles with little zest;
Refused, he found quick consolation;
Betrayed, was always glad to rest.
He sought them out with no elation
And left them too without vexation,
Scarce mindful of their love or spite.
Just so a casual guest at night
Drops in for whist and joins routinely;
And then upon the end of play,
Just takes his leave and drives away
To fall asleep at home serenely;
And in the morning he won't know
What evening holds or where he'll go.

11

But having read Tatyana's letter,
Onegin was profoundly stirred:
Her maiden dreams had helped unfetter
A swarm of thoughts with every word;
And he recalled Tatyana's pallor,
Her mournful air, her touching valour—
And then he soared, his soul alight
With sinless dreams of sweet delight.
Perhaps an ancient glow of passion
Possessed him for a moment's sway . . .
But never would he lead astray
A trusting soul in callous fashion.
And so let's hasten to the walk
Where he and Tanya had their talk.

12

Some moments passed in utter quiet,
And then Eugene approached and spoke:
'You wrote to me. Do not deny it.
I've read your words and they evoke
My deep respect for your emotion,
Your trusting soul . . . and sweet devotion.
Your candour has a great appeal
And stirs in me, I won't conceal,
Long dormant feelings, scarce remembered.
But I've no wish to praise you now;
Let me repay you with a vow
As artless as the one you tendered;
Hear my confession too, I plead,
And judge me both by word and deed.

13

'Had I in any way desired
To bind with family ties my life;
Or had a happy fate required
That I turn father, take a wife;
Had pictures of domestication
For but one moment held temptation—
Then, surely, none but you alone
Would be the bride I'd make my own.
I'll say without wrought-up insistence
That, finding my ideal in you,
I would have asked you—yes, it's true—
To share my baneful, sad existence,
In pledge of beauty and of good,
And been as happy . . . as I could!

14

'But I'm not made for exaltation:
My soul's a stranger to its call;
Your virtues are a vain temptation,
For I'm not worthy of them all.
Believe me (conscience be your token):
In wedlock we would both be broken.
However much I loved you, dear,
Once used to you . . . I'd cease, I fear;
You'd start to weep, but all your crying
Would fail to touch my heart at all,
Your tears in fact would only gall.
So judge yourself what we'd be buying,
What roses Hymen means to send—
Quite possibly for years on end!

15

'In all this world what's more perverted
Than homes in which the wretched wife
Bemoans her worthless mate, deserted—
Alone both day and night through life;
Or where the husband, knowing truly
Her worth (yet cursing fate unduly)
Is always angry, sullen, mute—
A coldly jealous, selfish brute!
Well, thus am I. And was it merely
For *this* your ardent spirit pined
When you, with so much strength of mind,
Unsealed your heart to me so clearly?
Can Fate indeed be so unkind?
Is this the lot you've been assigned?

16

'For dreams and youth there's no returning;
I cannot resurrect my soul.
I love you with a tender yearning,
But mine must be a brother's role.
So hear me through without vexation:
Young maidens find quick consolation—
From dream to dream a passage brief;
Just so a sapling sheds its leaf
To bud anew each vernal season.
Thus heaven wills the world to turn.
You'll fall in love again; but learn . . .
To exercise restraint and reason,
For few will understand you so,
And innocence can lead to woe.'

17

Thus spake Eugene his admonition.
Scarce breathing and bereft of speech,
Gone blind with tears, in full submission,
Tatyana listened to him preach.
He offered her his arm. Despairing,
She took it and with languid bearing
('Mechanically', as people say),
She bowed her head and moved away. . . .
They passed the garden's dark recesses,
Arriving home together thus—
Where no one raised the slightest fuss:
For country freedom too possesses
Its happy rights . . . as grand as those
That high and mighty Moscow knows.

18

I know that you'll agree, my reader,
That our good friend was only kind
And showed poor Tanya when he freed her
A noble heart and upright mind.
Again he'd done his moral duty,
But spiteful people saw no beauty
And quickly blamed him, heaven knows!
Good friends no less than ardent foes
(But aren't they one, if they offend us?)
Abused him roundly, used the knife.
Now every man has foes in life,
But from our friends, dear God, defend us!
Ah, friends, those friends! I greatly fear,
I find their friendship much too dear.

19

What's that? Just that. Mere conversation
To lull black empty thoughts awhile;
In passing, though, one observation:
There's not a calumny too vile—
That any garret babbler hatches,
And all the social rabble snatches;
There's no absurdity or worse,
Nor any vulgar gutter verse,
That your good friend won't find delightful,
Repeating it a hundred ways
To decent folk for days and days,
While never meaning to be spiteful;
He's yours, he'll say, through thick and thin:
He loves you so! . . . Why, you're like kin!

20

Hm, hm, dear reader, feeling mellow?
And are your kinfolk well today?
Perhaps you'd like, you gentle fellow,
To hear what I'm prepared to say
On 'kinfolk' and their implications?
Well, here's my view of close relations:
They're people whom we're bound to prize,
To honour, love, and idolize,
And, following the old tradition,
To visit come the Christmas feast,
Or send a wish by mail at least;
All other days they've our permission
To quite forget us, if they please—
So grant them, God, long life and ease!

21

Of course the love of tender beauties
Is surer far than friends or kin:
Your claim upon its joyous duties
Survives when even tempests spin.
Of course it's so. And yet be wary,
For fashions change, and views will vary,
And nature's made of wayward stuff—
The charming sex is light as fluff.
What's more, the husband's frank opinion
Is bound by any righteous wife
To be respected in this life;
And so your mistress (faithful minion)
May in a trice be swept away:
For Satan treats all love as play.

22

But whom to love? To trust and treasure?
Who won't betray us in the end?
And who'll be kind enough to measure
Our words and deeds as we intend?
Who won't sow slander all about us?
Who'll coddle us and never doubt us?
To whom will all our faults be few?
Who'll never bore us through and through?
You futile, searching phantom-breeder,
Why spend your efforts all in vain;
Just love yourself and ease the pain,
My most esteemed and honoured reader!
A worthy object! Never mind,
A truer love you'll never find.

23

But what ensued from Tanya's meeting?
Alas, it isn't hard to guess!
Within her heart the frenzied beating
Coursed on and never ceased to press
Her gentle soul, athirst with aching;
Nay, ever more intensely quaking,
Poor Tanya burns in joyless throes;
Sleep shuns her bed, all sweetness goes,
The glow of life has vanished starkly;
Her health, her calm, the smile she wore—
Like empty sounds exist no more,
And Tanya's youth now glimmers darkly:
Thus stormy shadows cloak with grey
The scarcely risen, newborn day.

24

Alas, Tatyana's fading quickly;
She's pale and wasted, doesn't speak!
Her soul, unmoved, grows wan and sickly;
She finds all former pleasures bleak.
The neighbours shake their heads morosely
And whisper to each other closely:
'It's time she married . . . awful waste. . . .'
But that's enough. I must make haste
To cheer the dark imagination
With pictures of a happy pair;
I can't, though, readers, help but care
And feel a deep commiseration;
Forgive me, but it's true, you know,
I love my dear Tatyana so!

25

Each passing hour more captivated
By Olga's winning, youthful charms,
Vladimir gave his heart and waited
To serve sweet bondage with his arms.
He's ever near. In gloomy weather
They sit in Olga's room together;
Or arm in arm they make their rounds
Each morning through the park and grounds.
And so? Inebriated lover,
Confused with tender shame the while
(Encouraged, though, by Olga's smile),
He sometimes even dares to cover
One loosened curl with soft caress
Or kiss the border of her dress.

26

At times he reads her works of fiction—
Some moralistic novel, say,
Whose author's powers of depiction
Make Chateaubriand's works seem grey;
But sometimes there are certain pages
(Outlandish things, mere foolish rages,
Unfit for maiden's heart or head),
Which Lensky, blushing, leaves unread. . . .
They steal away whenever able
And sit for hours seeing naught,
Above the chessboard deep in thought,
Their elbows propped upon the table;
Where Lensky with his pawn once took,
Bemused and muddled, his own rook.

27

When he drives home, she still engages
His poet's soul, his artist's mind;
He fills her album's fleeting pages
With every tribute he can find:
He draws sweet views of rustic scenery,
A Venus temple, graves and greenery;
He pens a lyre . . . and then a dove,
Adds colour lightly and with love;
And on the leaves of recollection,
Beneath the lines from other hands,
He plants a tender verse that stands—
Mute monument to fond reflection:
A moment's thought whose trace shall last
Unchanged when even years have passed.

28

I'm sure you've known provincial misses;
Their albums too you must have seen,
Where girlfriends scribble hopes and blisses—
From frontside, backside, in between.
With spellings awesome in abusage,
Unmetred lines of hallowed usage
Are entered by each would-be friend—
Diminished, lengthened, turned on end.
Upon the first page you'll discover:
Qu'écrirez-vous sur ces tablettes?
And 'neath it: *toute à vous Annette;*
While on the last one you'll uncover:
'Who loves you more than I must sign
And fill the page that follows mine.'

29

You're sure to find there decorations:
Rosettes, a torch, a pair of hearts;
You'll read, no doubt, fond protestations:
With all my love, till death us parts;
Some army scribbler will have written
A roguish rhyme to tease the smitten.
In just such albums, friends, I too
Am quite as glad to write as you,
For there, at heart, I feel persuaded
That any zealous vulgar phrase
Will earn me an indulgent gaze,
And won't then be evaluated
With wicked grin or solemn eye
To judge the wit with which I lie.

30

But you, odd tomes of haughty ladies,
You gorgeous albums stamped with gilt,
You libraries of darkest Hades
And racks where modish rhymesters wilt,
You volumes nimbly ornamented
By Tolstoy's* magic brush, and scented
By Baratynsky's pen—I vow:
Let God's own lightning strike you now!
Whenever dazzling ladies proffer
Their quartos to be signed by me,
I tremble with malicious glee;
My soul cries out and longs to offer
An epigram of cunning spite—
But madrigals they'll have you write!

31

No madrigals of mere convention
Does Olga's Lensky thus compose;
His pen breathes love, not pure invention
Or sparkling wit as cold as prose;
Whatever comes to his attention
Concerning Olga, *that* he'll mention;
And filled with truth's own vivid glows
A stream of elegies then flows.*
Thus you, Yazýkov,* with perfection,
With all the surgings of your heart,
Sing God knows whom in splendid art—
Sweet elegies, whose full collection
Will on some future day relate
The uncut story of your fate.

32

But hush! A strident critic rises
And bids us cast away the crown
Of elegy in all its guises
And to our rhyming guild calls down:
'Have done with all your lamentations,
Your endless croakings and gyrations
On "former days" and "times of yore";
Enough now! Sing of something more!'
You're right. And will you point with praises
To trumpet, mask, and dagger* too,
And bid us thuswise to renew
Our stock of dead ideas and phrases?
Is that it, friend?—'Far from it. Nay!
Write odes,* good sirs, write odes, I say . . .

33

'The way they did in former ages,
Those mighty years still rich in fame. . . .'
Just solemn odes? . . . On all our pages?!
Oh come now, friend, it's all the same.
Recall the satirist, good brother,
And his sly odist in *The Other*;*
Do you find him more pleasing, pray,
Than our glum rhymesters of today?. . . .
'Your elegy lacks all perception,
Its want of purpose is a crime;
Whereas the ode has aims sublime.'
One might to this take sharp exception,
But I'll be mute. I don't propose
To bring two centuries to blows.

34

By thoughts of fame and freedom smitten,
Vladimir's stormy soul grew wings;
What odes indeed he might have written,
But Olga didn't read the things.
How oft have tearful poets chances
To read their works before the glances
Of those they love? Good sense declares
That no reward on earth compares.
How blest, shy lover, to be granted
To read to her for whom you long:
The very object of your song,
A beauty languid and enchanted!
Ah, blest indeed . . . although it's true,
She may be dreaming not of you.

35

But I my fancy's fruits and flowers
(Those dreams and harmonies I tend)
Am quite content to read for hours
To my old nurse, my childhood's friend;
Or sometimes after dinners dreary,
When some good neighbour drops in weary—
I'll corner him and catch his coat
And stuff him with the play I wrote;
Or else (and here I'm far from jesting),
When off beside my lake I climb—
Beset with yearning and with rhyme—
I scare a flock of ducks from resting;
And hearing my sweet stanzas soar,
They flap their wings and fly from shore.

36*

And as I watch them disappearing,
A hunter hidden in the brush
Damns poetry for interfering
And, whistling, fires with a rush.
Each has his own preoccupation,
His favourite sport or avocation:
One aims a gun at ducks on high;
One is entranced by rhyme as I;
One swats at flies in mindless folly;
One dreams of ruling multitudes;
One craves the scent that war exudes;
One likes to bask in melancholy;
One occupies himself with wine:
And good and bad all intertwine.

37

But what of our Eugene this while?
Have patience, friends, I beg you, pray;
I'll tell it all in detailed style
And show you how he spent each day.
Onegin lived in his own heaven:
In summer he'd get up by seven
And, lightly clad, would take a stroll
Down to the stream below the knoll.
Gulnare's proud singer* his example,
He'd swim across this Hellespont;
Then afterwards, as was his wont,
He'd drink his coffee, sometimes sample
The pages of some dull review,
And then he'd dress. . . .

(38) 39

Long rambles, reading, slumber's blisses,
The burbling brook, the wooded shade,
At times the fresh and youthful kisses
Of white-skinned, dark-eyed country maid;
A horse of spirit fit to bridle,
A dinner fanciful and idle,
A bottle of some sparkling wine,
Seclusion, quiet—these, in fine,
Were my Onegin's saintly pleasures,
To which he yielded one by one,
Unmoved to count beneath the sun
Fair summer's days and careless treasures,
Unmindful too of town or friends
And their dull means to festive ends.

40

Our northern summers, though, are versions
Of southern winters, this is clear;
And though we're loath to cast aspersions,
They seem to go before they're here!
The sky breathed autumn, turned and darkled;
The friendly sun less often sparkled;
The days grew short and as they sped,
The wood with mournful murmur shed
Its wondrous veil to stand uncovered;
The fields all lay in misty peace;
The caravan of cackling geese
Turned south; and all around there hovered
The sombre season near at hand;
November marched across the land.

41

The dawn arises cold and cheerless;
The empty fields in silence wait;
And on the road . . . grown lean and fearless,
The wolf appears with hungry mate;
Catching the scent, the road horse quivers
And snorts in fear, the traveller shivers
And flies uphill with all his speed;
No more at dawn does shepherd need
To drive the cows outside with ringing;
Nor does his horn at midday sound
The call that brings them gathering round.
Inside her hut a girl is singing,
And by the matchwood's crackling light
She spins away the wintry night.

42

The frost already cracks and crunches;
The fields are silver where they froze . . .
(And you, good reader, with your hunches,
Expect the rhyme, so take it—Rose!)
No fine parquet could hope to muster
The ice-clad river's glassy lustre;
The joyous tribe of boys berates
And cuts the ice with ringing skates;
A waddling red-foot goose now scurries
To swim upon the water's breast;
He treads the ice with care to test . . .
And down he goes! The first snow flurries
Come flitting, flicking, swirling round
To fall like stars upon the ground.

43

But how is one, in this dull season,
To help the rural day go by?
Take walks? The views give little reason,
When only bareness greets the eye.
Go ride the steppe's harsh open spaces?
Your mount, if put to try his paces
On treacherous ice in blunted shoe,
Is sure to fall . . . and so will you.
So stay beneath your roof . . . try reading:
Here's Pradt* or, better, Walter Scott!
Or check accounts. You'd rather not?
Then rage or drink. . . . Somehow proceeding,
This night will pass (the next one too),
And grandly you'll see winter through!

44

Childe Harold-like, Onegin ponders,
Adrift in idle, slothful ways;
From bed to icy bath he wanders,
And then at home all day he stays,
Alone, and sunk in calculation,
His only form of recreation—
The game of billiards, all day through,
With just two balls and blunted cue.
But as the rural dusk encroaches,
The cue's forgot, the billiards fade;
Before the hearth the table's laid.
He waits. . . . At last his guest approaches:
It's Lensky's troika, three fine roans;
'Come on, let's dine, my stomach groans!'

45

Moët, that wine most blest and heady,
Or Veuve Cliquot, the finest class,
Is brought in bottle chilled and ready
And set beside the poet's glass.
Like Hippocrene* it sparkles brightly,
It fizzes, foams, and bubbles lightly
(A simile in many ways);
It charmed me too, in other days:
For its sake once, I squandered gladly
My last poor pence . . . remember, friend?
Its magic stream brought forth no end
Of acting foolish, raving madly,
And, oh, how many jests and rhymes,
And arguments, and happy times!

46

But all that foamy, frothy wheezing
Just plays my stomach false, I fear;
And nowadays I find more pleasing
Sedate Bordeaux's good quiet cheer.
Aï* I find is much too risky,
Aï is like a mistress—frisky,
Vivacious, brilliant . . . and too light.
But you, Bordeaux, I find just right;
You're like a comrade, ever steady,
Prepared in trials or in grief
To render service, give relief;
And when we wish it, always ready
To share a quiet evening's end.
Long live Bordeaux, our noble friend!

47

The fire goes out; the coal, still gleaming,
Takes on a film of ash and pales;
The rising vapours, faintly streaming,
Curl out of sight; the hearth exhales
A breath of warmth. The pipe smoke passes
Up chimney flue. The sparkling glasses
Stand fizzing on the table yet;
With evening's gloom, the day has set . . .
(I'm fond of friendly conversation
And of a friendly glass or two
At dusk or *entre chien et loup**—
As people say without translation,
Though why they do, I hardly know).
But listen as our friends speak low:

48

'And how are our dear neighbours faring?
Tatyana and your Olga, pray? . . .'
'Just half a glass, old boy, be sparing . . .
The family's well, I think I'd say;
They send you greetings and affection. . . .
Oh, God, my friend, what sheer perfection
In Olga's breast! What shoulders too!
And what a soul! . . . Come visit, do!
You ought to, really . . . they'll be flattered;
Or judge yourself how it must look—
You dropped in twice and closed the book;
Since then, it seems, they've hardly mattered.
In fact . . . Good Lord, my wits are bleak!
You've been invited there next week!'

49

'Tatyana's name-day celebration
Is Saturday. Her mother's sent
(And Olga too!) an invitation;
Now don't refuse, it's time you went.'
'There'll be a crush and lots of babble
And all that crowd of local rabble.'
'Why not at all, they just intend
To have the family, that's all, friend;
Come on, let's go, do *me* the favour!'
'Alright, I'll go.' 'Well done, first class!'
And with these words he drained his glass
In toast to his attractive neighbour . . .
And then waxed voluble once more
In talk of Olga. Love's a bore!

50

So Lensky soared as he awaited
His wedding day two weeks ahead;
With joy his heart anticipated
The mysteries of the marriage bed
And love's sweet crown of jubilations.
But Hymen's cares and tribulations,
The frigid, yawning days to be,
He never pictured once, not he.
While we, the foes of Hymen's banner,
Perceive full well that home life means
But one long string of dreary scenes—
In Lafontaine's* insipid manner.
But my poor Lensky, deep at heart,
Was born to play this very part.

51

Yes, he was loved . . . beyond deceiving . . .
Or so at least with joy he thought.
Oh, blest is he who lives believing,
Who takes cold intellect for naught,
Who rests within the heart's sweet places
As does a drunk in sleep's embraces,
Or as, more tenderly I'd say,
A butterfly in blooms of May;
But wretched he who's too far-sighted,
Whose head is never fancy-stirred,
Who hates all gestures, each warm word,
As sentiments to be derided,
Whose heart . . . experience has cooled
And barred from being loved . . . or fooled!

Chapter 5

Oh, never know these frightful dreams,
My dear Svetlana!

Zhukovsky

1

The fall that year was in no hurry,
And nature seemed to wait and wait
For winter. Then, in January,
The second night, the snow fell late.
Next day as dawn was just advancing,
Tatyana woke and, idly glancing,
Beheld outdoors a wondrous sight:
The roofs, the yard, the fence—all white;
Each pane a fragile pattern showing;
The trees in winter silver dyed,
Gay magpies on the lawn outside,
And all the hilltops soft and glowing
With winter's brilliant rug of snow—
The world all fresh and white below.

2

Ah, wintertime! . . . The peasant, cheerful,
Creates a passage with his sleigh;
Aware of snow, his nag is fearful,
But shambles somehow down the way.
A bold kibitka skips and burrows
And ploughs a trail of fluffy furrows;
The driver sits behind the dash
In sheepskin coat and scarlet sash.
And here's a household boy gone sleighing—
His *Blackie* seated on the sled,
While he plays horse and runs ahead;
The rascal froze his fingers, playing,
And laughs out loud between his howls,
While through the glass his mother scowls.

3

But you, perhaps, are not attracted
By pictures of this simple kind,
Where lowly nature is enacted
And nothing grand or more refined.
Warmed by the god of inspiration,
Another bard in exaltation
Has painted us the snow new-laid
And winter's joys in every shade.*
I'm sure you'll find him most engaging
When he, in flaming verse, portrays
Clandestine rides in dashing sleighs;
But I have no intent of waging
A contest for his crown . . . or thine,
Thou bard of Finland's maid divine!*

4

Tatyana (with a Russian duty
That held her heart, she knew not why)
Profoundly loved, in its cold beauty,
The Russian winter passing by:
Crisp days when sunlit hoarfrost glimmers,
The sleighs, and rosy snow that shimmers
In sunset's glow, the murky light
That wraps about the Yuletide night.
Those twelfthtide eves, by old tradition,
Were marked at home on their estate:
The servant maids would guess the fate
Of both young girls with superstition;
Each year they promised, as before,
Two soldier husbands and a war.

5

Tatyana heeded with conviction
All ancient folklore night and noon,
Believed in dreams and card prediction,
And read the future by the moon.
All signs and portents quite alarmed her,
All objects either scared or charmed her
With secret meanings they'd impart;
Forebodings filled and pressed her heart.
If her prim tomcat sat protected
Atop the stove to wash and purr,
Then this was certain sign to her
That guests were soon to be expected;
Or if upon her left she'd spy
A waxing crescent moon on high,

6

Her face would pale, her teeth would chatter.
Or when a shooting star flew by
To light the sombre sky and shatter
In fiery dust before her eye,
She'd hurry and, in agitation,
Before the star's disintegration,
Would whisper it her secret prayer.
Or if she happened anywhere
To meet a black-robed monk by error,
Or if amid the fields one day
A fleeing hare would cross her way,
She'd be quite overcome with terror,
As dark forebodings filled her mind
Of some misfortune ill defined.

7

Yet even in these same afflictions
She found a secret charm in part:
For nature—fond of contradictions—
Has so designed the human heart.
The holy days are here. What gladness! . . .
Bright youth divines, not knowing sadness,
With nothing that it must regret,
With all of life before it yet—
A distance luminous and boundless. . . .
Old age divines with glasses on
And sees the grave before it yawn,
All thoughts of time returning—groundless;
No matter: childish hope appears
To murmur lies in aged ears.

8

Tatyana watches, fascinated,
The molten wax submerge and turn
To wondrous shapes which designated
Some wondrous thing that she would learn.
Then from a basin filled with water
Their rings are drawn in random order;
When Tanya's ring turned up at last,
The song they sang was from the past:
'The peasants there have hoards of treasure,
They spade up silver from a ditch!
The one we sing to will be rich
And famous!' But the plaintive measure
Foretells a death to come ere long,
And girls prefer 'The Kitty's Song.'*

9

A frosty night, the sky resplendent
As heaven's galaxy shines down
And glides—so peaceful and transcendent. . . .
Tatyana, in her low-cut gown,
Steps out of doors and trains a mirror
Upon the moon to bring it nearer;*
But all that shows in her dark glass
Is just the trembling moon, alas. . . .
What's that . . . the crunching snow . . . who's coming?!
She flits on tiptoe with a sigh
And asks the stranger passing by,
Her voice more soft than reed pipe's humming:
'Oh, what's your name?' He hurries on,
Looks back and answers: 'Agafon.'*

10

Tatyana, as her nurse suggested,
Prepared to conjure all night through,*
And so in secret she requested
The bathhouse table laid for two.
But then sheer terror seized Tatyana . . .
And I, recalling poor Svetlana,*
Feel frightened too—so let it go,
We'll not have Tanya conjure so.
Instead, her silken sash untying,
She just undressed and went to bed.
Sweet Lel* now floats above her head,
While 'neath her downy pillow lying,
A maiden's looking-glass she keeps.
Now all is hushed. Tatyana sleeps.

11

And what an awesome dream she's dreaming:
She walks upon a snowy dale,
And all around her, dully gleaming,
Sad mist and murky gloom prevail;
Amid the drifting, snowbound spaces
A dark and seething torrent races,
A hoary frothing wave that strains
And tears asunder winter's chains;
Two slender, icebound poles lie linking
The chasm's banks atop the ridge:
A perilous and shaky bridge;
And full of doubt, her spirits sinking,
Tatyana stopped in sudden dread
Before the raging gulf ahead.

12

As at a vexing separation,
Tatyana murmured, at a loss;
She saw no friendly soul on station
To lend a hand to help her cross.
But suddenly a snowbank shifted,
And who emerged when it was lifted?
A huge and matted bear appeared!
Tatyana screamed! He growled and reared,
Then stretched a paw . . . sharp claws abhorrent,
To Tanya, who could barely stand;
She took it with a trembling hand
And worked her way across the torrent
With apprehensive step . . . then fled!
The bear just followed where she led.

13

She dare not look to see behind her,
And ever faster on she reels;
At every turn he seems to find her,
That shaggy footman at her heels! . . .
The grunting, loathesome bear still lumbers,
Before them now a forest slumbers;
The pines in all their beauty frown
And barely stir, all weighted down
By clumps of snow; and through the summits
Of naked linden, birch, and ash
The beams from heaven's lanterns flash;
There is no path; the gorge that plummets,
The shrubs, the land . . . all lie asleep,
By snowy blizzards buried deep.

14

She's reached the wood, the bear still tracking;
Soft snow, knee-deep, lies all about;
A jutting branch looms up, attacking,
And tears her golden earrings out;
And now another tries to trip her,
And from one charming foot her slipper,
All wet, comes off in crumbly snow;
And now she feels her kerchief go,
She lets it lie, she mustn't linger,
Behind her back she hears the bear,
But shy and frightened, does not dare
To lift her skirt with trembling finger;
She runs . . . but he keeps crashing on . . .
Until at last her strength is gone.

15

She sinks in snow; the bear alertly
Just picks her up and rushes on;
She lies within his arms inertly;
Her breathing stops, all sense is gone.
Along a forest road he surges,
And then, mid trees, a hut emerges;
Dense brush abounds; on every hand
Forlorn and drifting snowbanks stand;
A tiny window glitters brightly,
And from the hut come cries and din;
The bear proclaims: 'My gossip's in.'
'Come warm yourself,' he adds politely,
Then pushes straightway through the door
And lays her down upon the floor.

16

On coming to, she looks around her:
She's in a hall; no bear at least;
The clink of glasses, shouts . . . confound her,
As if it were some funeral feast;
She can't make sense of what she's hearing,
Creeps to the door and, softly peering,
Sees through a crack the strangest thing—
A horde of monsters in a ring:
Out of a dog-face horns are sprouting;
One has a rooster's head on top;
A goateed witch is on a mop;
A haughty skeleton sits pouting
Beside a short-tailed dwarf . . . and *that*
Is half a crane and half a cat.

17

More wondrous still and still more fearful:
A crab upon a spider sat;
On goose's neck a skull seemed cheerful,
While spinning round in bright red hat;
A windmill there was squat-jig dancing
And cracked and waved its sails while prancing;
Guffawing, barking, whistles, claps,
And human speech and hoofbeat taps!
But what was Tanya's stunned reaction
When mid the guests she recognized
The one she feared, the one she prized—
The hero of our novel's action!
Onegin sits amid the roar
And glances slyly through the door.

18

He gives a sign—the others hustle;
He drinks—all drink and all grow shrill;
He laughs—they all guffaw and bustle;
He frowns—and all of them grow still.
He's master here, there's no mistaking;
And Tanya, now no longer quaking,
Turns curious to see still more
And pushes slightly on the door. . . .
The sudden gust of wind surprises
The band of goblins, putting out
The night-time lanterns all about;
His eyes aflame, Onegin rises
And strikes his chair against the floor;
All rise; he marches to the door.

19

And fear assails her; in a panic
She tries to flee . . . but feels too weak;
In anguished writhing, almost manic,
She wants to scream . . . but cannot speak;
Eugene throws wide the door, revealing
To monstrous looks and hellish squealing
Her slender form; fierce cackles sound
In savage glee; all eyes turn round,
All hooves and trunks—grotesque and curving,
And whiskers, tusks, and tufted tails,
Red bloody tongues and snouts and nails,
Huge horns and bony fingers swerving—
All point at her and all combine
To shout as one: 'She's mine! She's mine!'

20

'She's mine!' announced Eugene, commanding;
And all the monsters fled the room;
The maid alone was left there standing
With *him* amid the frosty gloom.
Onegin stares at her intently,
Then draws her to a corner gently
And lays her on a makeshift bed,
And on her shoulder rests his head. . . .
Then Olga enters in confusion,
And Lensky too; a light shines out;
Onegin lifts an arm to rout
Unbidden guests for their intrusion;
He rants at them, his eyes turn dread;
Tatyana lies there nearly dead.

21

The heated words grow louder, quicken;
Onegin snatches up a knife,
And Lensky falls; the shadows thicken;
A rending cry amid the strife
Reverberates . . . the cabin quivers;
Gone numb with terror, Tanya shivers . . .
And wakes to find her room alight,
The frozen windows sparkling bright,
Where dawn's vermilion rays are playing;
Then Olga pushes through the door,
More rosy than the dawn before
And lighter than a swallow, saying:
'Oh, tell me, do, Tatyana love,
Who was it you were dreaming of?'

22

But she ignores her sister's pleading,
Just lies in bed without a word,
Keeps leafing through some book she's reading,
So wrapt in thought she hasn't heard.
Although the book she read presented
No lines a poet had invented,
No sapient truths, no pretty scenes—
Yet neither Virgil's, nor Racine's,
Nor Seneca's, nor Byron's pages,
Nor even *Fashion Plates Displayed*
Had ever so engrossed a maid:
She read, my friends, that king of sages
Martýn Zadéck,* Chaldean seer
And analyst of dreams unclear.

23

This noble and profound creation
A roving pedlar one day brought
To show them in their isolation,
And finally left it when they bought
*Malvina** for three roubles fifty
(A broken set, but he was thrifty);
And in exchange he also took
Two Petriads,* a grammar book,
Some fables he could sell tomorrow,
Plus Marmontel*—just volume three.
Martýn Zadéck soon came to be
Tatyana's favourite. Now when sorrow
Assails her heart, he brings her light,
And sleeps beside her through the night.

24

Her dream disturbs her, and not knowing
What secret message she'd been sent,
Tatyana seeks some passage showing
Just what the dreadful vision meant.
She finds in alphabetic order
What clues the index can afford her:
There's bear and blizzard, bridge, and crow,
Fir, forest, hedgehog, night, and snow,
And many more. But her confusion
Martýn Zadéck cannot dispel;
The frightful vision must foretell
Sad times to come and disillusion.
For several days she couldn't find
A way to calm her troubled mind.

25

But lo! . . . with crimson hand Aurora
Leads forth from morning dales the sun*
And brings in merry mood before her
The name-day feast that's just begun.
Since dawn Dame Larin's near relations
Have filled the house; whole congregations
Of neighbour clans have come in drays,
Kibitkas, britzkas, coaches, sleighs.
The hall is full of crowds and bustle;
The drawing room explodes with noise,
With bark of pugs and maidens' joys,
With laughter, kisses, din and hustle;
The guests all bow and scrape their feet,
Wet nurses shout and babies bleat.

26

Fat Pustyakóv, the local charmer,
Has come and brought his portly wife;
Gvozdín as well, that model farmer,
Whose peasants lead a wretched life;
The two Skotínins, grey as sages,
With children of all shapes and ages—
From two to thirty at the top;
Here's Petushkóv, the district fop;
And my first cousin, good Buyánov,*
Lint-covered, in his visored cap
(As you, of course, well know the chap);
And former couns'lor, old man Flyánov,
A rogue and gossip night and noon,
A glutton, grafter, and buffoon.

27

The Harlikóvs were feeling mellow
And brought along Monsieur Triquet,
Late from Tambóv, a witty fellow
In russet wig and fine pince-nez.
True Gaul, Triquet in pocket carried
A verse to warn that Tanya tarried,
Set to a children's melody:
*Réveillez-vous, belle endormie.**
The printed verse had lain neglected
In some old tattered almanac
Until Triquet, who had a knack
For rhyme, saw fit to resurrect it
And boldly put for 'belle Niná'
The charming line: 'belle Tatyaná.'*

28

And now from nearby quarters, brothers,
That idol whom ripe misses cheer,
The joy and hope of district mothers—
The company commander's here!
He's brought some news to set them cheering:
The regimental band's appearing!
'The colonel's sending it tonight.'
There'll be a ball! What sheer delight!
The girls all jump and grow excited.
But dinner's served. And so by pairs,
And arm in arm, they seek their chairs:
The girls near Tanya; men delighted
To face them; and amid the din,
All cross themselves and dig right in.

29

Then for a moment chatter ceases
As mouths start chewing. All around
The clink of plates and forks increases,
The glasses jingle and resound.
But soon the guests are somewhat sated;
The hubbub grows more animated . . .
But no one hears his neighbour out;
All laugh and argue, squeal and shout.
The doors fly back; two figures enter—
It's Lensky . . . with Eugene! 'Oh dear!'
The hostess cries, 'At last you're here!'
The guests all squeeze toward the centre,
Each moves his setting, shifts his chair,
And in a trice they seat the pair.

30

Across from Tanya—there they place them;
And paler than the moon at dawn,
She cannot raise her eyes to face them
And trembles like a hunted fawn.
Inside her, stormy passion's seething;
The wretched girl is scarcely breathing;
The two friends' greetings pass unheard;
Her tears well up without a word
And almost fall; the poor thing's ready
To faint; but deep within her, will
And strength of mind were working still,
And they prevailed. Her lips more steady,
She murmured something through her pain
And managed somehow to remain.

31

All tragico-hysteric moaning,
All girlish fainting-fits and tears,
Had long since set Eugene to groaning:
He'd borne enough in former years.
Already cross and irritated
By being at this feast he hated,
And noting how poor Tanya shook,
He barely hid his angry look
And fumed in sullen indignation;
He swore that he'd make Lensky pay
And be avenged that very day.
Exulting in anticipation,
He inwardly began to draw
Caricatures of those he saw.

32

Some others too might well have noted
Poor Tanya's plight; but every eye
Was at the time in full devoted
To sizing up a lavish pie*
(Alas, too salty); now they're bringing,
In bottle with the pitch still clinging,
Between the meat and *blancmanger*,
Tsimlyánsky wine . . . a whole array
Of long-stemmed glasses . . . (quite as slender
As your dear waist, my sweet Zizí,*
Fair crystal of my soul and key
To all my youthful verses tender,
Love's luring phial, you who once
Made me a drunken, love-filled dunce!)

33

The bottle pops as cork goes flying;
The fizzing wine comes gushing fast;
And now with solemn mien, and dying
To have his couplet heard at last,
Triquet stands up; the congregation
Falls silent in anticipation.
Tatyana's scarce alive; Triquet,
With verse in hand, looks Tanya's way
And starts to sing, off-key. Loud cheering
And claps salute him. Tanya feels
Constrained to curtsey . . . almost reels.
The bard, whose modesty's endearing,
Is first to toast her where he stands,
Then puts his couplet in her hands.

34

Now greetings come, congratulations;
Tatyana thanks them for the day;
But when Eugene's felicitations
Came due in turn, the girl's dismay,
Her weariness and helpless languor,
Evoked his pity more than anger:
He bowed to her in silence, grave . . .
But somehow just the look he gave
Was wondrous tender. If asserting
Some feeling for Tatyana's lot,
Or if, unconsciously or not,
He'd only teased her with some flirting,
His look was still a tender dart:
It reawakened Tanya's heart.

35

The chairs, pushed back, give out a clatter;
The crowd moves on to drawing room:
Thus bees from luscious hive will scatter,
A noisy swarm, to meadow bloom.
Their festive dinner all too pleasing,
The squires face each other wheezing;
The ladies to the hearth repair;
The maidens whisper by the stair;
At green-baize tables players settle,
As Boston, ombre (old men's play),
And whist, which reigns supreme today,
Call out for men to try their mettle:
A family with a single creed,
All sons of boredom's endless greed.

36

Whist's heroes have by now completed
Eight rubbers; and eight times as well
They've shifted round and been reseated;
Now tea is brought. I like to tell
The time of day by teas and dinners,
By supper's call. We country sinners
Can tell the time without great fuss:
The stomach serves as clock for us;
And apropos, I might make mention
In passing that I speak as much
Of feasts and foods and corks and such
In these odd lines of my invention—
As you, great Homer, you whose song
Has lasted thirty centuries long!

(37–8) 39

But tea is brought: the girls demurely
Have scarcely taken cups in hand,
When suddenly from ballroom doorway
Bassoon and flute announce the band.
Elated by the music's bouncing,
His tea and rum at once renouncing,
That Paris of the local towns,
Good Petushkóv, to Olga bounds;
To Tanya, Lensky; Harlikóva,
A maiden somewhat ripe in glow,
My Tambov poet takes in tow;
Buyánov whirls off Pustyakóva;
Then all the crowd comes pouring in
To watch the brilliant ballroom spin.

40

At the beginning of my story
(In Chapter One, if you recall),
I wanted with Albani's glory*
To paint a Petersburg grand ball;
But then, by empty dreams deflected,
I lost my way and recollected
The feet of ladies known before.
In your slim tracks I'll stray no more,
O charming feet and mad affliction!
My youth betrayed, it's time to show
More common sense if I'm to grow,
To mend my ways in deeds and diction,
And cleanse this Chapter Five at last
Of all digressions from the past.

41

Monotonous and mad procession,
Young life's own whirlwind, full of sound,
Each pair a blur in quick succession,
The rousing waltz goes whirling round.
His moment of revenge beginning,
Eugene, with secret malice grinning,
Approaches Olga . . . idly jests,
Then spins her round before the guests;
He stays beside her when she's seated,
Proceeds to talk of this and that;
Two minutes barely has she sat . . .
And then their waltzing is repeated!
The guests all stare in mute surprise;
Poor Lensky can't believe his eyes.

42

Now the mazurka's call is sounded.
Its thunder once could even rack
The greatest hall when it resounded,
And under heels parquet would crack;
The very windows shook like Hades.
But now it's changed: we're all like ladies;
And o'er the lacquered boards we glide.
But in small town and countryside
The old mazurka hasn't faltered;
It still retains its pristine joys:
Moustaches, leaps, heel-pounding noise
Remain the same; they've not been altered
By tyrant-fashion's high decrees,
The modern Russian's new disease.

(43) 44

My bold Buyánov guides expertly
Tatyana to our hero's side,
And Olga too; Eugene alertly
Makes off with Lensky's future bride.
He steers her, gliding nonchalantly,
And bending, whispers her gallantly
Some common madrigal to please,
Then gives her hand a gentle squeeze;
She blushes in appreciation,
Her prim conceited face alight,
While Lensky rages at the sight.
Consumed with jealous indignation,
He waits till the mazurka's through,
Then asks her for the dance he's due.

45

But no, she can't. What explanation? . . .
Well, she's just promised his good friend
The next dance too. In God's creation!
What's this he hears? Could she intend? . . .
Can this be real? Scarce more than swaddler—
And turned coquette! A fickle toddler!
Already has she mastered guile,
Already learned to cheat and smile!
The blow has left poor Lensky shattered;
And cursing woman's crooked course,
He leaves abruptly, calls for horse,
And gallops off. Now nothing mattered—
A brace of pistols and a shot
Shall instantly decide his lot.

Chapter 6

La sotto i giorni nubilosi e brevi,
Nasce una gente, a cui l'morir non dole.*

Petrarch

1

Though pleased with the revenge he'd taken,
Onegin, noting Lensky'd left,
Felt all his old ennui awaken,
Which made poor Olga feel bereft.
She too now yawns and, as she dances,
Seeks Lensky out with furtive glances;
The endless dance had come to seem
To Olga like some dreadful dream.
But now it's over. Supper's heeded.
Then beds are made; the guests are all
Assigned their rooms—from entrance hall
To servants' quarters. Rest is needed
By everyone. Eugene has fled
And driven home alone to bed.

2

All's quiet now. Inside the parlour,
The portly Mr. Pustyakóv
Lies snoring with his portly partner.
Gvozdín, Buyánov, Petushkóv—
And Flyánov, who'd been reeling badly—
On dining chairs have bedded gladly;
While on the floor Triquet's at rest
In tattered nightcap and his vest.
The rooms of Olga and Tatyana
Are filled with girls in sleep's embrace.
Alone, beside the windowcase,
Illumined sadly by Diana,
Poor Tanya, sleepless and in pain,
Sits gazing at the darkened plain.

3

His unexpected reappearance,
That momentary tender look,
The strangeness of his interference
With Olga—all confused and shook
Tatyana's soul. His true intention
Remained beyond her comprehension,
And jealous anguish pierced her breast—
As if a chilling hand had pressed
Her heart; as if in awful fashion
A rumbling, black abyss did yawn. . . .
'I'll die,' she whispers to the dawn,
'But death from him is sweet compassion.
Why murmur vainly? He can't give
The happiness for which I live.'

4

But forward, forward, O my story!
A new persona has arrived:
Five versts or so from Krasnogory,
Our Lensky's seat, there lived and thrived
In philosophical seclusion
(And does so still, have no illusion)
Zarétsky—once a rowdy clown,
Chief gambler and arch rake in town,
The tavern tribune and a liar—
But now a kind and simple soul
Who plays an unwed father's role,
A faithful friend, a peaceful squire,
And man of honour, nothing less:
Thus does our age its sins redress!

5

Time was, when flunkies in high places
Would praise him for his nasty grit:
He could, it's true, from twenty paces,
Shoot pistol at an ace and hit;
And once, when riding battle station,
He'd earned a certain reputation
When in a frenzied state indeed
He'd plunged in mud from Kalmuk steed,
Drunk as a pig, and suffered capture
(A prize to make the French feel proud!).
Like noble Regulus,* he bowed,
Accepting hostage bonds with rapture—
In hopes that he (on charge) might squeeze
Three bottles daily from Véry's.*

6

He used to banter rather neatly,
Could gull a fool, and had an eye
For fooling clever men completely,
For all to see, or on the sly;
Of course not all his pranks succeeded
Or passed unpunished or unheeded,
And sometimes he himself got bled
And ended up the dunce instead.
He loved good merry disputations,
Could answer keenly, be obtuse,
Put silence cunningly to use,
Or cunningly start altercations;
Could get two friends prepared to fight,
Then lead them to the duelling site;

7

Or else he'd patch things up between them
So he might lunch with them as guest,
And later secretly demean them
With nasty gossip or a jest. . . .
Sed alia tempora! Such sporting
(With other capers such as courting)
Goes out of us when youth is dead—
And my Zaretsky, as I've said,
Neath flow'ring cherries and acacias,
Secure at last from tempest's rage,
Lives out his life a proper sage,
Plants cabbages like old Horatius,
Breeds ducks and geese, and oversees
His children at their ABCs.

8

He was no fool; and consequently
(Although he thought him lacking heart),
Eugene would hear his views intently
And liked his common sense in part.
He'd spent some time with him with pleasure,
And so was not in any measure
Surprised next morning when he found,
Zaretsky had again called round;
The latter, hard upon first greeting,
And cutting off Eugene's reply,
Presented him, with gloating eye,
The poet's note about a 'meeting'.
Onegin, taking it, withdrew
And by the window read it through.

9

The note was brief in its correctness,
A proper challenge or *cartel*:
Politely, but with cold directness,
It called him out and did it well.
Onegin, with his first reaction,
Quite curtly offered satisfaction
And bade the envoy, if he cared,
To say that he was *quite prepared*.
Avoiding further explanation,
Zaretsky, pleading much to do,
Arose . . . and instantly withdrew.
Eugene, once left to contemplation
And face to face with his own soul,
Felt far from happy with his role.

10

And rightly so: in inquisition,
With conscience as his judge of right,
He found much wrong in his position:
First off, he'd been at fault last night
To mock in such a casual fashion
At tender love's still timid passion;
And why not let the poet rage!
A fool, at eighteen years of age,
Can be excused his rash intentions.
Eugene, who loved the youth at heart,
Might well have played a better part—
No plaything of the mob's conventions
Or brawling boy to take offence,
But man of honour and of sense.

11

He could have shown some spark of feeling
Instead of bristling like a beast;
He should have spoken words of healing,
Disarmed youth's heart . . . or tried at least.
'Too late,' he thought, 'the moment's wasted. . . .
What's more, that duelling fox has tasted
His chance to mix in this affair—
That wicked gossip with his flair
For jibes . . . and all his foul dominion.
He's hardly worth contempt, I know,
But fools will whisper . . . grin . . . and crow! . . .'
So there it is—the mob's opinion!
The spring with which our honour's wound!
The god that makes this world go round!

12

At home the poet, seething, paces
And waits impatiently to hear.
Then *in* his babbling neighbour races,
The answer in his solemn leer.
The jealous poet's mood turned festive!
He'd been, till now, uncertain . . . restive,
Afraid the scoundrel might refuse
Or laugh it off and, through some ruse,
Escape unscathed . . . the slippery devil!
But now at last his doubts were gone:
Next day, for sure, they'd drive at dawn
Out to the mill, where each would level
A pistol, cocked and lifted high,
To aim at temple or at thigh.

13

Convinced that Olga's heart was cruel,
Vladimir vowed he wouldn't run
To see that flirt before the duel.
He kept consulting watch and sun . . .
Then gave it up and finally ended
Outside the door of his intended.
He thought she'd blush with self-reproach,
Grow flustered when she saw his coach;
But not at all: as blithe as ever,
She bounded from the porch above
And rushed to greet her rhyming love
Like giddy hope—so gay and clever,
So frisky-carefree with her grin,
She seemed the same she'd always been.

14

'Why did you leave last night so early?'
Was all that Olga, smiling, said.
Poor Lensky's muddled mind was swirling,
And silently he hung his head.
All jealousy and rage departed
Before that gaze so openhearted,
Before that soft and simple trust,
Before that soul so bright and just!
With misty eyes he looks on sweetly
And sees the truth: *she loves him yet*!
Tormented now by deep regret,
He craves her pardon so completely,
He trembles, hunts for words in vain:
He's happy now, he's almost sane. . . .

(15–16) 17

Once more in solemn, rapt attention
Before his darling Olga's face,
Vladímir hasn't heart to mention
The night before and what took place;
'It's up to me,' he thought, 'to save her.
I'll never let that foul depraver
Corrupt her youthful heart with lies,
With fiery praise . . . and heated sighs;
Nor see that noxious worm devour
My lovely lily, stalk and blade;
Nor watch this two–day blossom fade
When it has yet to fully flower.'
All this, dear readers, meant in fine:
I'm duelling with a friend of mine.

18

Had Lensky known the deep emotion
That seared my Tanya's wounded heart!
Or had Tatyana had some notion
Of how these two had grown apart,
Or that by morn they'd be debating,
For which of them the grave lay waiting!—
Ah, then, perhaps, the love she bore
Might well have made them friends once more!
But no one knew her inclination
Or chanced upon the sad affair.
Eugene had kept his silent air;
Tatyana pined in isolation;
And only nanny might have guessed,
But her old wits were slow at best.

19

All evening Lensky was abstracted,
Remote one moment, gay the next;
But those on whom the Muse has acted
Are ever thus; with brow perplexed,
He'd sit at clavichord intently
And play but chords; or turning gently
To Olga, he would whisper low:
'I'm happy, love . . . it's true, you know.'
But now it's late and time for leaving.
His heart, so full of pain, drew tight;
And as he bid the girl goodnight,
He felt it break with desperate grieving.
'What's wrong?' She peered at him, intent.
'It's nothing.' And away he went.

20

On coming home, the youth inspected
His pistols; then he put them back.
Undressed, by candle he selected
A book of Schiller's from the rack;
But only one bright image holds him,
One thought within his heart enfolds him:
He sees before him, wondrous fair,
His incandescent Olga there.
He shuts the book and, with decision,
Takes up his pen. . . . His verses ring
With all the nonsense lovers sing;
And feverish with lyric vision,
He reads them out like one possessed,
Like drunken Delvig* at a fest!

21

By chance those verses haven't vanished;
I have them, and I quote them here:
'Ah, whither, whither are ye banished,
My springtime's golden days so dear?
What fate will morning bring my lyre?
In vain my searching eyes enquire,
For all lies veiled in misty dust.
No matter; fate's decree is just;
And whether, pierced, I fall anointed,
Or arrow passes by—all's right:
The hours of waking and of night
Come each in turn as they're appointed;
And blest with all its cares the day,
And blest the dark that comes to stay!

22

'The morning star will gleam tomorrow,
And brilliant day begin to bloom;
While I, perhaps, descend in sorrow
The secret refuge of the tomb. . . .
Slow Lethe, then, with grim insistence,
Will drown my memory's brief existence;
Of me the world shall soon grow dumb;
But thou, fair maiden, wilt thou come!
To shed a tear in desolation
And think at my untimely grave:
He loved me and for me he gave
His mournful life in consecration! . . .
Beloved friend, sweet friend, I wait,
Oh, come, Oh, come, I am thy mate!'

23

He wrote thus—*limply and obscurely*.
(We say 'romantically'—although,
That's not romanticism, surely;
And if it is, who wants to know?)
But then at last, as it was dawning,
With drooping head and frequent yawning,
Upon the modish word 'ideal'
Vladimir gently dozed for real;
But sleep had hardly come to take him
Off to be charmed by dreams and cheered,
When in that silent room appeared
His neighbour, calling out to wake him:
'It's time to rise! Past six . . . come on!
I'll bet Onegin woke at dawn.'

24

But he was wrong; that idle sinner
Was sleeping soundly even then.
But now the shades of night grow thinner,
The cock hails Vesper once again;
Yet still Onegin slumbers deeply.
But now the sun climbs heaven steeply,
And gusting snowflakes flash and spin,
But still Onegin lies within
And hasn't stirred; still slumber hovers
Above his bed and holds him fast.
But now he slowly wakes at last,
Draws back the curtains and his covers,
Looks out—and sees with some dismay,
He'd better leave without delay.

25

He rings in haste and, with a racket,
His French valet, Guillot, runs in—
With slippers and a dressing jacket,
And fresh new linen from the bin.
Onegin, dressing in a flurry,
Instructs his man as well to hurry:
They're leaving for the duelling place,
Guillot's to fetch the pistol case.
The sleigh's prepared; his pacing ceases;
He climbs aboard and off they go.
They reach the mill. He bids Guillot
To bring Lepage's deadly pieces;*
Then has the horses, on command,
Removed to where two oaklings stand.

26

Impatient, but in no great panic,
Vladimir waited near the dam;
Meanwhile Zaretsky, born mechanic,
Was carping at the millstone's cam.
Onegin, late, made explanation.
Zaretsky frowned in consternation:
'Good God, man, where's your second? Where?'
In duels a purist doctrinaire,
Zaretsky favoured stout reliance
On proper form; he'd not allow
Dispatching chaps just anyhow,
But called for strict and full compliance
With rules, traditions, ancient ways
(Which we, of course, in him should praise).

27

'My second?' said Eugene directly.
'Why here he is: Monsieur Guillot,
A friend of mine, whom you . . . *correctly*!
Will be quite pleased to greet, I know;
Though he's unknown and lives obscurely,
He's still an honest chap, most surely.'
Zaretsky bit his lip, well vexed.
Onegin turned to Lensky next:
'Shall we begin?'—'At my insistence.'
Behind the mill, without a word.
And while the 'honest chap' conferred
With our Zaretsky at a distance
And sealed the solemn compact fast,
The foes stood by with eyes downcast.

28

The foes! How long has bloodlust parted
And so estranged these former friends?
How long ago did they, warmhearted,
Share meals and pastimes, thoughts and ends?
And now, malignant in intention,
Like ancient foes in mad dissension,
As in a dreadful senseless dream,
They glower coldly as they scheme
In silence to destroy each other. . . .
Should they not laugh while yet there's time,
Before their hands are stained with crime?
Should each not part once more as brother? . . .
But enmity among their class
Holds shame in savage dread, alas.

29

The gleaming pistols wake from drowsing.
Against the ramrods mallets pound.
The balls go in each bevelled housing.
The first sharp hammer clicks resound.
Now streams of greyish powder settle
Inside the pans. Screwed fast to metal,
The jagged flints are set to go.
Behind a nearby stump Guillot
Takes up his stand in indecision.
The duellists shed their cloaks and wait.
Zaretsky paces off their fate
At thirty steps with fine precision,
Then leads each man to where he'll stand,
And each takes pistol into hand.

30

'Approach at will!' Advancing coldly,
With quiet, firm, and measured tread,
Not aiming yet, the foes took boldly
The first four steps that lay ahead—
Four fateful steps. The space decreasing,
Onegin then, while still not ceasing
His slow advance, was first to raise
His pistol with a level gaze.
Five paces more, while Lensky waited
To close one eye and, only then,
To take his aim. . . . And that was when
Onegin fired! The hour fated
Has struck at last: the poet stops
And silently his pistol drops.

31

He lays a hand, as in confusion,
On breast and falls. His misted eyes
Express not pain, but death's intrusion.
Thus, slowly, down a sloping rise,
And sparkling in the sunlight's shimmer,
A clump of snow will fall and glimmer.
Eugene, in sudden chill, despairs,
Runs to the stricken youth . . . and stares!
Calls out his name!—No earthly power
Can bring him back: the singer's gone,
Cut down by fate at break of dawn!
The storm has blown; the lovely flower
Has withered with the rising sun;
The altar fire is out and done! . . .

32

He lay quite still and past all feeling;
His languid brow looked strange at rest.
The steaming blood poured forth, revealing
The gaping wound beneath his breast.
One moment back—a breath's duration—
This heart still throbbed with inspiration;
Its hatreds, hopes, and loves still beat,
Its blood ran hot with life's own heat.
But now, as in a house deserted,
Inside it—all is hushed and stark,
Gone silent and forever dark.
The window boards have been inserted,
The panes chalked white. The owner's fled;
But where, God knows. All trace is dead.

33

With epigrams of spite and daring
It's pleasant to provoke a foe;
It's pleasant when you see him staring—
His stubborn, thrusting horns held low—
Unwillingly within the mirror,
Ashamed to see himself the clearer;
More pleasant yet, my friends, if he
Shrieks out in stupid shock: that's me!
Still pleasanter is mute insistence
On granting him his resting place
By shooting at his pallid face
From some quite gentlemanly distance.
But once you've had your fatal fun,
You won't be pleased to see it done.

34

And what would be your own reaction
If with your pistol you'd struck down
A youthful friend for some infraction:
A bold reply, too blunt a frown,
Some bagatelle when you'd been drinking;
Or what if he himself, not thinking,
Had called you out in fiery pride?
Well, tell me: what would you . . . inside
Be thinking of . . . or merely feeling,
Were your good friend before you now,
Stretched out with death upon his brow,
His blood by slow degrees congealing,
Too deaf and still to make reply
To your repeated, desperate cry?

35

In anguish, with his heart forsaken,
The pistol in his hand like lead,
Eugene stared down at Lensky, shaken.
His neighbour spoke: 'Well then, he's dead.'
The awful word, so lightly uttered,
Was like a blow. Onegin shuddered,
Then called his men and walked away.
Zaretsky, carefully, then lay
The frozen corpse on sleigh, preparing
To drive the body home once more.
Sensing the dreadful load they bore,
The horses neighed, their nostrils flaring,
And wet the metal bit with foam,
Then swift as arrows raced for home.

36

You mourn the poet, friends . . . and rightly:
Scarce out of infant clothes and killed!
Those joyous hopes that bloomed so brightly
Now doomed to wither unfulfilled!
Where now the ardent agitation,
The fine and noble aspiration
Of youthful feeling, youthful thought,
Exalted, tender, boldly wrought?
And where are stormy love's desires,
The thirst for knowledge, work, and fame,
The dread of vice, the fear of shame?
And where are you, poetic fires,
You cherished dreams of sacred worth
And pledge of life beyond this earth!

37

It may be he was born to fire
The world with good, or earn at least
A gloried name; his silenced lyre
Might well have raised, before it ceased,
A call to ring throughout the ages.
Perhaps, upon the world's great stages,
He might have scaled a lofty height.
His martyred shade, condemned to night,
Perhaps has carried off forever
Some sacred truth, a living word,
Now doomed by death to pass unheard;
And in the tomb his shade shall never
Receive our race's hymns of praise,
Nor hear the ages bless his days.

(38) 39

Or maybe he was merely fated
To live amid the common tide;
And as his years of youth abated,
The flame within him would have died.
In time he might have changed profoundly,
Have quit the Muses, married soundly;
And in the country he'd have worn
A quilted gown and cuckold's horn,
And happy, he'd have learned life truly;
At forty he'd have had the gout,
Have eaten, drunk, grown bored and stout,
And so decayed, until he duly
Passed on in bed . . . his children round,
While women wept and doctors frowned.

40

However, reader, we may wonder . . .
The youthful lover's voice is stilled,
His dreams and songs all rent asunder;
And he, alas, by friend lies killed!
Not far from where the youth once flourished
There lies a spot the poet cherished:
Two pine trees grow there, roots entwined;
Beneath them quiet streamlets wind,
Meand'ring from the nearby valley.
And there the ploughman rests at will
And women reapers come to fill
Their pitchers in the stream and dally;
There too, within a shaded nook,
A simple stone adjoins the brook.

41

Sometimes a shepherd sits there waiting
(Till on the fields, spring rains have passed)
And sings of Volga fishers, plaiting
His simple, coloured shoes of bast;
Or some young girl from town who's spending
Her summer in the country mending—
When headlong and alone on horse
She races down the meadow course,
Will draw her leather reins up tightly
To halt just there her panting steed;
And lifting up her veil, she'll read
The plain inscription, skimming lightly;
And as she reads, a tear will rise
And softly dim her gentle eyes.

42

And at a walk she'll ride, dejected,
Into the open field to gaze,
Her soul, despite herself, infected
By Lensky's brief, ill-fated days.
She'll wonder too: 'Did Olga languish?
Her heart consumed with lasting anguish?
Or did the time of tears soon pass?
And where's her sister now, poor lass?
And where that gloomy, strange betrayer,
The modish beauty's modish foe,
That recluse from the world we know—
The youthful poet's friend and slayer?'
In time, I promise, I'll not fail
To tell you all in full detail.

43

But not today. Although I cherish
My hero and of course I vow
To see how he may wane or flourish,
I'm not quite in the mood just now.
The years to solemn prose incline me;
The years chase playful rhyme behind me,
And I—alas, I must confess—
Pursue her now a good deal less.
My pen has lost its disposition
To mar the fleeting page with verse;
For other, colder dreams I nurse,
And sterner cares now seek admission;
And mid the hum and hush of life,
They haunt my soul with dreams of strife.

44

I've learned the voice of new desires
And come to know a new regret;
The first within me light no fires,
And I lament old sorrows yet.
O dreams! Where has your sweetness vanished?
And where has youth (glib rhyme) been banished?
Can it be true, its bloom has passed,
Has withered, withered now at last?
Can it be true, my heyday's ended—
All elegiac play aside—
That now indeed my spring has died
(As I in jest so oft pretended)?
And is there no return of youth?
Shall I be thirty soon, in truth?

45

And so, life's afternoon has started,
As I must now admit, I see.
But let us then as friends be parted,
My sparkling youth, before you flee!
I thank you for your host of treasures,
For pain and grief as well as pleasures,
For storms and feasts and worldly noise,
For all your gifts and all your joys;
My thanks to you. With you I've tasted,
Amid the tumult and the still,
Life's essence . . . and enjoyed my fill.
Enough! Clear-souled and far from wasted,
I start upon an untrod way
To take my rest from yesterday.

46

But one glance back. Farewell, you bowers,
Sweet wilderness in which I spent
Impassioned days and idle hours,
And filled my soul with dreams, content.
And you, my youthful inspiration,
Come stir the bleak imagination,
Enrich the slumbering heart's dull load,
More often visit my abode;
Let not the poet's soul grow bitter
Or harden and congeal alone,
To turn at last to lifeless stone
Amid this world's deceptive glitter,
This swirling swamp in which we lie
And wallow, friends, both you and I!

Chapter 7

Moscow! Russia's favourite daughter!
Where is your equal to be found!

Dmitriev

Can one not love our native Moscow?

Baratynsky

'Speak ill of Moscow! So this is what it means
to see the world! Where is it better, then?'
'Where we are not.'

Griboedov

1

Spring rays at last begin to muster
And chase from nearby hills the snow,
Whose turbid streams flow down and cluster
To inundate the fields below.
And drowsy nature, smiling lightly,
Now greets the dawning season brightly.
The heavens sparkle now with blue;
The still transparent woods renew
Their downy green and start to thicken.
The bee flies out from waxen cell
To claim its meed from field and dell.
The vales grow dry and colours quicken;
The cattle low; and by the moon
The nightingale pours forth its tune.

2

How sad I find your apparition,
O spring! . . . O time of love's unrest!
What sombre echoes of ambition
Then stir my blood and fill my breast!
What tender and oppressive yearning
Possesses me on spring's returning,
When in some quiet rural place
I feel her breath upon my face!
Or am I now inured to gladness;
And all that quickens and excites,
That sparkles, triumphs, and delights
Casts only spleen and languid sadness
On one whose heart has long been dead,
For whom but darkness lies ahead?

3

Or saddened by the re-emergence
Of leaves that perished in the fall,
We heed the rustling wood's resurgence,
As bitter losses we recall;
Or do we mark with lamentation
How nature's lively renovation
Compares with our own fading youth,
For which no spring will come, in truth?
Perhaps in thought we reassemble,
Within a dream to which we cling,
Some other and more ancient spring,
That sets the aching heart atremble
With visions of some distant place,
A magic night, the moon's embrace. . . .

4

Now is the time, you hibernators,
You epicures and sages, you;
You fortunate procrastinators,
You fledglings from our Lyóvshin's crew,*
You rustic Priams from the cities,
And you, my sentimental pretties—
Spring calls you to your country seat;
It's time for flowers, labours, heat,
Those heady walks for which you're thirsting,
And soft seductive nights as well.
Into the fields, my friends, pell-mell!
Load up your carriages to bursting,
Bring out your own or rent a horse,
And far from town now set your course!

5

You too, indulgent reader, hurry
In your imported coach, I pray,
To leave the city with its flurry,
Where you spent wintertime in play;
And with my wilful Muse let's hustle
To where the leafy woodlands rustle—
A nameless river's placid scene,
The country place where my Eugene,
That idle and reclusive schemer,
But recently this winter stayed,
Not far from our unhappy maid,
Young Tanya, my enchanted dreamer;
But where he now no longer reigns . . .
Where only his sad trace remains.

6

Where hills half circle round a valley,
Let's trace a winding brooklet's flow
Through greening fields, and watch it dally
Beside a spot where lindens grow.
And there the nightingale, spring's lover,
Sings out till dawn; a crimson cover
Of briar blooms, and freshets sound.
There too a tombstone can be found
Beneath two pine trees, old for ages.
Its legend lets the stranger know:
'Vladímir Lensky lies below.
He died too soon . . . his death courageous,
At such an age, in such a year.
Repose in peace, young poet, here!'

7

There was a time when breezes playing
Among the pines would gently turn
A secret wreath that hung there swaying
Upon a bough above that urn;
And sometimes in the evening hours
Two maidens used to come with flowers,
And by the moonlit grave they kept
Their vigil and, embracing, wept.
But now the monument stands dreary
And quite forgot. Its pathway now—
All weeds. No wreath is on the bough;
Alone the shepherd, grey and weary,
Beneath it sings as in the past
and plaits his simple shoes of bast.

(8–9) 10

My poor, poor Lensky! Yes, she mourned him;
Although her tears were all too brief!
Alas! His fiancée has scorned him
And proved unfaithful to her grief.
Another captured her affection,
Another with his love's perfection
Has lulled her wretchedness to sleep:
A lancer has enthralled her deep,
A lancer whom she loves with passion;
And at the altar by his side,
She stands beneath the crown a bride,
Her head bent down in modest fashion,
Her lowered eyes aflame the while,
And on her lips a slender smile.

11

Poor Lensky! In his place of resting,
In deaf eternity's grim shade,
Did he, sad bard, awake protesting
The fateful news, he'd been betrayed?
Or lulled by Lethe, has he slumbered,
His blissful spirit unencumbered
By feelings and perturbed no more,
His world a closed and silent door?
Just so! The tomb that lies before us
Holds but oblivion in the end.
The voice of lover, foe, and friend
Falls silent fast. Alone the chorus
Of angry heirs in hot debate
Contests obscenely our estate.

12

Soon Olga's happy voice and beauty
No longer cheered the family group.
A captive of his lot and duty,
Her lancer had to join his troop.
Dame Larin's eyes began to water
As she embraced her younger daughter
And, scarce alive, cried out goodbye.
But Tanya found she couldn't cry;
A deathly pallor merely covered
Her stricken face. When all came out
Onto the porch and fussed about
While taking leave, Tatyana hovered
Beside the couple's coach below,
Then sadly saw the lovers go.

13

And long she watched the road they'd taken,
As through a mist of stifled tears. . . .
Now Tanya is alone, forsaken!
Companion of so many years,
The darling sister whom she'd nourished,
The bosom friend she'd always cherished—
Now carried off by fate, a bride,
Forever parted from her side.
She roams in aimless desolation,
Now gazes at the vacant park. . . .
But all seems joyless, bleak and dark;
There's nothing offers consolation
Or brings her smothered tears relief;
Her heart is rent in two by grief.

14

And in the solitude her passion
Burns even stronger than before,
Her heart speaks out in urgent fashion
Of faraway Eugene the more.
She'll never see him . . . and be grateful,
She finds a brother's slayer hateful
And loathes the awful thing he's done.
The poet's gone . . . and hardly one
Remembers him; his bride's devotion
Has flown to someone else instead;
His very memory now has fled
Like smoke across an azure ocean.
Two hearts, perhaps, remain forlorn
And mourn him yet. . . . But wherefore mourn?

15

'Twas evening and the heavens darkled.
A beetle hummed. The peasant choirs
Were bound for home. Still waters sparkled.
Across the river, smoky fires
Of fishermen were dimly gleaming.
Tatyana walked, alone and dreaming,
Beneath the moonbeams' silver light
And climbed a gentle hill by night.
She walked and walked . . . till with a shiver
She spied a distant hamlet's glow,
A manor house and grove below,
A garden by the glinting river.
And as she gazed upon that place
Her pounding heart began to race.

16

Assailed by doubts, she grew dejected:
'Should I go on, turn back, or what?
He isn't here, I'm not expected. . . .
I'll glance at house and garden plot.'
And so, scarce breathing, down she hastened
And looked about, perplexed and chastened
To find herself at his estate. . . .
She entered the deserted gate.
A pack of barking dogs chased round her;
And at her frightened cry a troop
Of household urchins with a whoop
Came rushing quickly to surround her.
They made the barking hounds obey,
Then led the lady, safe, away.

17

'May I just see the house, I wonder?'
Asked Tanya . . . and the children leapt
To find Anísya and to plunder
The household keys she always kept.
Anísya came in just a second,
And soon the open doorway beckoned.
She stepped inside the empty shell
Where once our hero used to dwell.
She found a cue left unattended
Upon the table after play,
And on a rumpled sofa lay
His riding crop. And on she wended.
'And here's the hearth,' spoke up the crone,
'Where master used to sit alone.

18

'Our neighbour Lensky, lately buried,
Would dine with him in winter here.
Come this way, please . . . but don't feel hurried.
And here's the master's study, dear;
He slept, took coffee in these quarters,
Would hear the bailiff, give his orders,
And mornings read some book right through. . . .
My former master lived here too;
On Sundays at his window station,
His glasses on, he'd deign to play
Some cards with me to pass the day.
God grant his mortal soul salvation,
And may his dear old bones be blest
In Mother Earth where he's at rest.'

19

Tatyana looks in melting pleasure
At everything around the room;
She finds it all a priceless treasure,
A painful joy that lifts her gloom
And leaves her languid soul ignited:
The desk, the lamp that stands unlighted,
The heap of books, the carpet spread
Before the window on the bed,
That semi-light, so pale and solemn,
The view outdoors—the lunar pall,
Lord Byron's portrait on the wall,
The iron bust* upon its column—
With clouded brow beneath a hat,
The arms compressed and folded flat.

20

And long she stood, bewitched and glowing,
Inside that modish bachelor cell.
But now it's late. The winds are blowing,
It's cold and dark within the dell.
The grove's asleep above the river,
Behind the hill the moon's a sliver;
And now it's time, indeed long past,
That our young pilgrim leave at last.
Concealing her wrought-up condition,
Though not without a heartfelt sigh,
Tatyana turns to say goodbye,
But, taking leave, requests permission
To see the vacant house alone
And read the books he'd called his own.

21

Outside the gate Tatyana parted
From old Anísya. Next day then,
She rose at dawn and off she started
To see the empty house again;
And once inside that silent study,
Sealed off at last from everybody,
The world for just a time forgot,
Tatyana wept and mourned her lot . . .
Then turned to see the books he'd favoured.
At first she didn't wish to read,
The choice of books seemed strange indeed;
But soon her thirsting spirit savoured
The mystery that those pages told—
And watched a different world unfold.

22

Although Onegin's inclination
For books had vanished, as we know,
He did exempt from condemnation
Some works and authors even so:
The bard of Juan and the Giaour,*
And some few novels done with power,
In which our age is well displayed
And modern man himself portrayed
With something of his true complexion—
With his immoral soul disclosed,
His arid vanity exposed,
His endless bent for deep reflection,
His cold, embittered mind that seems
To waste itself in empty schemes.

23

Some pages still preserved the traces
Where fingernails had sharply pressed;
The girl's attentive eye embraces
These lines more quickly than the rest.
And Tanya sees with trepidation
The kind of thought or observation
To which Eugene paid special heed,
Or where he'd tacitly agreed.
And in the margins she inspected
His pencil marks with special care;
And on those pages everywhere
She found Onegin's soul reflected—
In crosses or a jotted note,
Or in the question mark he wrote.

24

And so, in slow but growing fashion
My Tanya starts to understand
More clearly now—thank God—her passion
And him for whom, by fate's command,
She'd been condemned to feel desire:
That dangerous and sad pariah,
That work of heaven or of hell,
That angel . . . and proud fiend as well.
What was he then? An imitation?
An empty phantom or a joke,
A Muscovite in Harold's cloak,
Compendium of affectation,
A lexicon of words in vogue . . .
Mere parody and just a rogue?

25

Can she have solved the riddle's power?
Can she have found the final clue?
She hardly notes how late the hour,
And back at home she's overdue—
Where two old friends in conversation
Speak out on Tanya's situation:
'What *can* I do? Tatyana's grown,'
Dame Larin muttered with a moan.
'Her younger sister married neatly;
It's time that she were settled too,
I swear I don't know *what* to do;
She turns all offers down completely,
Just says: "I can't", then broods away,
And wanders through those woods all day.'

26

'Is she in love?'—'With whom, I wonder?
Buyánov tried: she turned him down.
And Petushkóv as well went under.
Pykhtín the lancer came from town
To stay with us and seemed transported;
My word, that little devil courted!
I thought she might accept him then;
But no! the deal fell through again.'
'Why, my dear lady, what's the bother?
To Moscow and the marriage mart!
They've vacancies galore . . . take heart!'
'But I've so little income, father.'
'Sufficient for one winter's stay;
Or borrow then—from me, let's say.'

27

The good old lady was delighted
To hear such sensible advice;
She checked her funds and then decided,
A Moscow winter would be nice.
Tatyana heard the news morosely—
The haughty world would watch her closely
And judge her harshly from the start:
Her simple, open country heart
And country dress would find no mercy;
And antiquated turns of phrase
Were sure to bring a mocking gaze
From every Moscow fop and Circe!
O horrors! No, she'd better stay
Safe in her woods and never stray.

28

With dawn's first rays Tatyana races
Out to the open fields to sigh;
And gazing softly, she embraces
The world she loves and says goodbye:
'Farewell, my peaceful vales and fountains!
Farewell, you too, familiar mountains
And woods where once I used to roam!
Farewell, celestial beauty's home,
Farewell, fond nature, where I flourished!
I leave your world of quiet joys
For empty glitter, fuss, and noise!
Farewell, my freedom, deeply cherished!
Oh, where and why do I now flee?
And what does Fate prepare for me?'

29

And all that final summer season
Her walks were long; a brook or knoll
Would stop her now for no good reason
Except to charm her thirsting soul.
As with old friends, she keeps returning
To all her groves and meadows, yearning
To talk once more and say goodbye.
But quickly summer seems to fly,
The golden autumn now arriving.
Now nature, tremulous, turns pale—
A victim draped in lavish veil. . . .
The North now howls, the winds are driving
The clouds before them far and near:
That sorceress the winter's here!

30

She's spread herself through field and fountain,
And hung the limbs of oaks with white;
She lies atop the farthest mountain
In wavy carpets glistening bright;
She's levelled with a fluffy blanket
Both river and the shores that flank it.
The frost has gleamed, and we give thanks
For Mother Winter's happy pranks.
But Tanya's heart is far from captured:
She doesn't greet the winter's glow,
Inhale the frostdust, gather snow
From bathhouse roof to wash, enraptured,
Her shoulders, face, and breast. With dread
She views the winter path ahead.

31

Departure day was long expected;
The final hours come at last.
The covered sleigh, for years neglected,
Is checked, relined, and soon made fast.
The usual three-cart train will carry
What household goods are necessary:
The mattresses, the trunks and chairs,
Some jars of jam and kitchen wares,
The featherbeds and coops of chickens,
Some pots and basins, and the rest—
Well, almost all that they possessed.
The servants fussed and raised the dickens
About the stable, many cried;
Then eighteen nags were led outside.

32

They're harnessed to the coach and steadied;
The cooks make lunch for one and all;
The heaped-up wagons now are readied;
The wenches and the drivers brawl.
Atop a lean and shaggy trotter
The bearded postboy sits as spotter.
Retainers crowd the gate pell-mell
To bid their mistresses farewell.
They're all aboard and, slowly gliding,
The ancient coach creeps out the gate.
'Farewell, my peaceful home and fate!
Farewell, secluded place of hiding!
Shall I return?' And Tanya sighs,
As tears well up to dim her eyes.

33

When we have broadened education,
The time will come without a doubt
(By scientific computation,
Within five hundred years about),
When our old roads' decayed condition
Will change beyond all recognition.
Paved highways, linking every side,
Will cross our Russia far and wide;
Above our waters iron bridges
Will stride in broadly arching sweep;
We'll dig bold tunnels 'neath the deep
And even part whole mountain ridges;
And Christendom will institute
An inn at every stage *en route*.

34

But roads are bad now in our nation;
Neglected bridges rot and fall;
Bedbugs and fleas at every station
Won't let the traveller sleep at all.
No inns exist. At posting stages
They hang pretentious menu pages,
But just for show, as if to spite
The traveller's futile appetite;
While some rude Cyclops at his fire
Treats Europe's dainty artefacts
With mighty Russian hammer whacks,
And thanks the Lord for ruts and mire
And all the ditches that abound
Throughout our native Russian ground.

35

And yet a trip in winter season
Is often easy, even nice.
Like modish verse devoid of reason,
The winter road is smooth as ice.
Our bold Autómedons* stay cheery,
Our Russian troikas never weary;
And mileposts soothe the idle eye
As fencelike they go flashing by.
Unluckily, Dame Larin wasted
No funds on renting fresher horse,
Which meant a longer trip of course;
And so our maiden fully tasted
Her share of travel's dull delights:
They rode for seven days and nights.

36

But now they're near. Before them, gleaming,
Lies Moscow with its stones of white,
Its ancient domes and spires streaming
With golden crosses, ember-bright.
Ah, friends, I too have been delighted
When all at once far-off I've sighted
That splendid view of distant domes,
Of churches, belfries, stately homes!
How oft . . . forlorn and separated—
When wayward fate has made me stray—
I've dreamt of Moscow far away!
Ah, Moscow! How that sound is freighted
With meaning for our Russian hearts!
How many echoes it imparts!

37

And here's Petróvsky Castle,* hoary
Amid its park. In sombre dress
It wears with pride its recent glory:
Napoleon, drunk with fresh success,
Awaited here, in vain, surrender—
For kneeling Moscow's hand to tender
The ancient Kremlin's hallowed keys.
But Moscow never bent her knees,
Nor bowed her head in subjugation;
No welcome feast did she prepare
The restless hero waiting there—
But lit instead a conflagration.
From here he watched, immersed in thought,
The awesome blaze my Moscow wrought.

38

Farewell now, scene of fame unsteady,
Petróvsky Castle. Hey! Be fleet!
There gleam the city gates already!
And now along Tverskáya Street
The sleigh glides over ruts and passes
By sentry booths and peasant lasses;
By gardens, mansions, fashion shops;
Past urchins, streetlamps, strolling fops,
Bokhárins, sleighs, apothecaries,
Muzhíks and merchants, Cossack guards;
Past towers, hovels, boulevards,
Great balconies and monasteries;
Past gateway lions' lifted paws,
And crosses dense with flocks of daws.

(39) 40

This tiring trek through town extended
For two full hours; then, quite late
Nearby St Chariton's it ended
Before a mansion's double gate.
For now they'll seek accommodation
With Tanya's aunt, a kind relation—
Four years consumptive, sad to note.
In glasses and a torn old coat,
A grizzled Kalmuk came to meet them;
With sock in hand he led the way
To where the prostrate princess lay;
She called from parlour couch to greet them.
The two old ladies hugged and cried,
With shouts of joy on either side.

41

'*Princesse, mon ange!*' 'Pachette!' 'Oh, Laura!'
'Who would have thought?' 'How long it's been!'
'I hope you'll stay?' 'Dear cousin Laura!'
'Sit down. . . . How strange! . . . I can't begin . . .
I'd swear it's from some novel's pages!'
'And here's my Tanya.' 'Lord, it's ages!
Oh, Tanya sweet, come over here—
I think I must be dreaming, dear. . . .
Oh, cousin, do you still remember
Your Grandison?' 'I never knew . . .
Oh, *Grandison!* . . . of course I do!'
'He lives in Moscow. This December,
On Christmas eve, he paid a call:
He married off his son this fall.

42

'The other. . . . But we'll talk tomorrow;
And straightway too, to all her kin
We'll show your Tanya. What a sorrow
That paying visits does me in;
I drag about like some poor laggard.
But here, your trip has left you haggard;
Let's all go have a nice long rest. . . .
I've got no strength . . . this weary breast
Finds even joy at times excessive,
Not only woe. . . . It's true, my dear,
I'm good for nothing now, I fear;
When one gets old, life turns oppressive.'
And all worn out, she wept a bit,
Then broke into a coughing fit.

43

The sick old lady's kindly smile
Left Tanya moved; but she felt sad
Within this strange new domicile
And missed the room she'd always had.
In bed, beneath her silken curtain,
She lies there sleepless and uncertain;
And early church bells—when they chime,
Announcing dawn and working time—
Rouse Tanya from her bed to listen.
She sits before the windowsill.
The darkness wanes, but Tanya still
Can't see her fields and valleys glisten:
She sees an unknown yard instead:
A stable, fence, and kitchen shed.

44

And now they trundle Tanya daily
To family dinners just to share
With grandams and granduncles gaily
Her languid and abstracted air.
Those kin who've come from distant places
Are always met with warm embraces,
With shouts of joy and welcome cheer.
'How Tanya's grown! It seems, my dear,
So short a time since I baptized you!'
'And since I dried your baby tears!'
'And since I pulled you by the ears!'
'And since my gingerbread surprised you!'
And with one voice the grannies cry:
'Good gracious, how the years do fly!'

45

In *them*, though, nothing ever alters;
The same old patterns still are met:
Old Aunt Eléna never falters
And wears that same tulle bonnet yet;
Still powdered is Lukérya Lvóvna;
A liar still, Lyubóv Petróvna;
Iván Petróvich . . . no more bright;
Semyón Petróvich . . . just as tight;
And Anna Pávlovna, as ever,
Still has her friend, Monsieur Finemouch,
Her same old spouse, and same old pooch—
Her husband, clubman come whatever,
Is just as meek and deaf, it's true,
And still consumes enough for two.

46

Their daughters, after brief embraces,
Look Tanya over good and slow;
In silence Moscow's youthful graces
Examine her from head to toe.
They find her stranger than expected,
A bit provincial and affected,
And somewhat pale, too thin and small,
But on the whole, not bad at all;
Then bowing to innate compassion,
They squeeze her hand and, in the end,
Take Tanya in and call her friend;
They fluff her curls in latest fashion,
And in their singsong tones impart
Their girlish secrets of the heart—

47

Both others' and their own successes,
Their hopes, and pranks, and maiden dreams;
All innocence, their talk progresses—
Though now and then some gossip gleams.
And then they ask, in compensation
For their sweet flow of revelation,
For *her* confessions of romance.
But Tanya, in a kind of trance,
Attends their giddy conversation
Without response and takes no part;
And all the while she guards her heart
With silence and in meditation:
Her cherished trove of tears and bliss
She'll share with none, aloud like this.

48

Tatyana tries to pay attention
When in the parlour guests converse;
But all they ever seem to mention
Is incoherent rot, or worse;
They seem so pallid and so weary,
And even in their slander dreary.
In all the sterile words they use—
In arid gossip, questions, news—
Not once all day does thought but flicker,
Not even in some chance remark;
The languid mind will find no spark,
The heart no cause to beat the quicker;
And even simple-minded fun
This hollow world has learned to shun!

49

'Archival dandies'* in a cluster
Eye Tanya with a priggish frown,
And with their usual sort of bluster,
Among themselves they put her down.
One melancholy joker found her
His 'true ideal' and hovered round her—
Then, leaning by the door, prepared
An elegy, to show he cared.
Once Vyázemsky* sat down beside her
(On meeting her at some dull aunt's)
And managed to dispel her trance;
And some old man—when he espied her—
Put straight his wig and asked around
About this unknown belle he'd found.

50

But where Melpomene still stages
Her stormy scenes and wails aloud
And in her gaudy mantle rages
Before the dull and frigid crowd;
Where sweet Thalia calmly dozes,
Indifferent to admirers' roses;
Where just Terpsichore enchants
The youthful lover of the dance
(As was the case—for nothing passes—
In our day too, let's not forget),
No jealous lady trained lorgnette,
No modish connoisseur his glasses,
To spy on Tanya down below
From boxes rising row on row.

51

They take her to the Grand Assembly:*
And there the crush, the glare, the heat,
The music's roar, the ballroom trembling,
The whirling flash of pairs of feet,
The beauties in their filmy dresses,
The swarming gallery throng that presses,
The host of girls on marriage hunts—
Assault the senses all at once.
Here practised dandies bow and slither
To show their gall . . . and waistcoats too,
With negligent lorgnettes in view.
Hussars on leave come racing hither
To strut their stuff and thunder by,
To dazzle, conquer . . . and to fly.

52

The night has countless stars to light her,
And Moscow countless beauties too;
And yet the regal moon shines brighter
Than all her friends in heaven's blue;
And she, whose beauty I admire—
But dare not bother with my lyre—
Just like the moon upon her throne,
Mid wives and maidens shines alone.
With what celestial pride she grazes
The earth she walks, in splendour dressed!
What languor fills her lovely breast!
How sensuous her wondrous gazes! . . .
But there, enough; have done at last:
You've paid your due to follies past.

53

Commotion, bows . . . the glad, the solemn . . .
Galop, mazurka, waltz. . . . And there,
Between two aunts, beside a column,
Observed by none, and near despair,
Tatyana looks with eyes unseeing
And loathes this world with all her being;
She's stifled here . . . and in her mind
Calls up the life she left behind—
The countryside, poor village neighbours,
A distant and secluded nook
Beside a limpid flowing brook,
Her flowers, novels, daily labours . . .
That dusky, linden-shaded walk
Where *he* and she once had their talk.

54

And so, far off in thought she wandered:
The *monde*, the noisy ball forgot;
But all the while, as Tanya pondered,
Some general stared her way a lot.
The aunts exchanged a wink and nodded,
And with an elbow each one prodded
Tatyana, whisp'ring in her ear:
'Look quickly to your left, my dear.'
'My left? But why? It seems like gawking.'
'Just never mind . . . now look up there . . .
That group in front; you see that pair . . .
In uniform? The one not talking . . .
He just moved off. . . . He's turning round.'
'That heavy general?' Tanya frowned.

55

But here let's honour with affection
My Tanya's conquest taking wing,
And steer for now a new direction,
Lest I forget of whom I sing—
On which, herewith, these observations:
I sing strange whims and aberrations,
I sing a youthful friend of mine.
O Muse of Epics, may you shine
On my long work as I grow older!
And armed with your good staff, I pray,
May I not roam too far astray.
Enough! The burden's off my shoulder!
To classicism I've been true:
The foreword's here, if overdue.

Chapter 8

Fare thee well, and if for ever,
Still for ever, fare thee well.

Byron

1

In days when I still bloomed serenely
Inside our Lycée* garden wall
And read my Apuleius keenly,
But read no Cicero at all—
Those springtime days in secret valleys,
Where swans call out and beauty dallies,
Near waters sparkling in the still,
The Muse first came to make me thrill.
My student cell turned incandescent;
And there the Muse spread out for me
A feast of youthful fancies free,
And sang of childhood effervescent,
The glory of our days of old,
The trembling dreams the heart can hold.

2

And with a smile the world caressed us;
What wings our first successes gave!
The old Derzhávin* saw—and blessed us,
As he descended to the grave.

.   .   .   .

3

And I, who saw my single duty
As heeding passion's siren song—
To share with all the world her beauty,
Would take my merry Muse along
To rowdy feasts and altercations—
The bane of midnight sentry stations;
And to each mad and fevered rout
She brought her gifts . . . and danced about,
Bacchante-like, at all our revels,
And over wine she sang for guests;
And in those days when I was blest,
The young pursued my Muse like devils;
While I, mid friends, was drunk with pride—
My flighty mistress at my side.

4

But from that band I soon departed—
And fled afar . . . and she as well.
How often, on the course I charted,
My gentle Muse's magic spell
Would light the way with secret stories!
How oft, mid far Caucasia's glories,
Like fair Lenore,* on moonlit nights
She rode with me those craggy heights!
How often on the shores of Tauris,*
On misty eves, she led me down
To hear the sea's incessant sound,
The Nereids'* eternal chorus—
That endless chant the waves unfurled
In praise of him who made the world.

5

Forgetting, then, the city's splendour,
Its noisy feasts and grand events,
In sad Moldavia she turned tender
And visited the humble tents
Of wandering tribes; and like a child,
She learned their ways and soon grew wild:
The language of the gods she shed
For strange and simple tongues instead—
To sing the savage steppe,* elated;
But then her course abruptly veered,
And in my garden* she appeared—
A country miss—infatuated,
With mournful air and brooding glance,
And in her hands a French romance.

6

And now I seize the first occasion
To show my Muse a grand soirée;
I watch with jealous trepidation
Her rustic charms on full display.
And lo! my beauty calmly passes
Through ranks of men from highborn classes,
Past diplomats and soldier–fops,
And haughty dames . . . then calmly stops
To sit and watch the grand procession—
The gowns, the talk, the milling mass,
The slow parade of guests who pass
Before the hostess in succession,
The sombre men who form a frame
Around each painted belle and dame.

7

She likes the stately disposition
Of oligarchic colloquies,
Their chilly pride in high position,
The mix of years and ranks she sees.
But who is that among the chosen,
That figure standing mute and frozen,
That stranger no one seems to know?
Before him faces come and go
Like spectres in a bleak procession.
What is it—martyred pride, or spleen
That marks his face? . . . Is that Eugene? !
That figure with the strange expression?
Can that be he? It is, I say.
'But when did fate cast him our way?

8

'Is he the same, or is he learning?
Or does he play the outcast still?
In what new guise is he returning?
What role does he intend to fill?
Childe Harold? Melmoth for a while?
Cosmopolite? A Slavophile?
A Quaker? Bigot?—might one ask?
Or will he sport some other mask?
Or maybe he's just dedicated,
Like you and me, to being nice?
In any case, here's my advice:
Give up a role when it's outdated.
He's gulled the world . . . now let it go.'
'You know him then?' 'Well, yes and no.'

9

But why on earth does he inspire
So harsh and negative a view?
Is it because we never tire
Of censuring what others do?
Because an ardent spirit's daring
Appears absurd or overbearing
From where the smug and worthless sit?
Because the dull are cramped by wit?
Because we take mere talk for action,
And malice rules a petty mind?
Because in tripe the solemn find
A cause for solemn satisfaction,
And mediocrity alone
Is what we like and call our own?

10

Oh, blest who in his youth was tender;
And blest who ripened in his prime;
Who learned to bear, without surrender,
The chill of life with passing time;
Who never knew exotic visions,
Nor scorned the social mob's decisions;
Who was at twenty fop or swell,
And then at thirty, married well,
At fifty shed all obligation
For private and for other debts;
Who gained in turn, without regrets,
Great wealth and rank and reputation;
Of whom lifelong the verdict ran:
'Old X is quite a splendid man.'

11

How sad that youth, with all its power,
Was given us in vain, to burn;
That we betrayed it every hour,
And were deceived by it in turn;
That all our finest aspirations,
Our brightest dreams and inspirations,
Have withered with each passing day
Like leaves dank autumn rots away.
It's hard to face a long succession
Of dinners stretching out of sight,
To look at life as at a rite,
And trail the seemly crowd's procession—
Indifferent to the views they hold,
And to their passions ever cold.

12

When one becomes the butt of rumour,
It's hard to bear (as you well know)
When men of reason and good humour
Perceive you as a freak on show,
Or as a sad and raving creature,
A monster of Satanic feature,
Or even Demon of my pen!*
Eugene (to speak of him again),
Who'd killed his friend for satisfaction,
Who in an aimless, idle fix
Had reached the age of twenty-six,
Annoyed with leisure and inaction,
Without position, work, or wife—
Could find no purpose for his life.

13

He felt a restless, vague ambition,
A craving for a change of air
(A most unfortunate condition—
A cross not many choose to bear).
He left his home in disillusion
And fled the woods' and fields' seclusion,
Where every day before his eyes
A bloody spectre seemed to rise;
He took up travel for distraction,
A single feeling in his breast;
But journeys too, like all the rest,
Soon proved a wearisome attraction.
So he returned one day to fall,
Like Chatsky,* straight from boat to ball.

14

But look, the crowd's astir and humming;
A murmur through the ballroom steals . . .
The hostess sees a lady coming,
A stately general at her heels.
She isn't hurried or obtrusive,
Is neither cold nor too effusive;
She casts no brazen glance around
And makes no effort to astound
Or use those sorts of affectation
And artifice that ladies share—
But shows a simple, quiet air.
She seems the very illustration
Du comme il faut . . . (Shishkov,* be kind:
I can't translate this phrase, I find.)

15

The ladies flocked to stand beside her;
Old women beamed as she went by;
The men bowed lower when they spied her
And sought in vain to catch her eye;
Young maidens hushed in passing by her;
While none held head and shoulders higher
Than he who brought the lady there—
The general with the prideful air.
One couldn't label her a beauty;
But neither did her form contain,
From head to toe, the slightest strain
Of what, with fashion's sense of duty,
The London social sets decry
As *vulgar*. (I won't even try

16

To find an adequate translation
For this delicious epithet;
With us the word's an innovation,
But though it's won no favour yet,
'Twould make an epigram of style.* . . .
But where's our lady all this while?)
With carefree charm and winsome air
She took a seat beside the chair
Of brilliant Nina Voronskáya,*
That Cleopatra of the North;
But even Nina, shining forth
With all her marble beauty's fire—
However dazzling to the sight—
Could not eclipse her neighbour's light.

17

'Can it be true?' Eugene reflected.
'Can that be she? . . . It seems . . . and yet . . .
From those backwoods!' And he directed
A curious and keen lorgnette
For several minutes in succession
Upon the lady whose expression
Called up a face from long ago.
'But tell me, Prince, you wouldn't know
Who's standing there in conversation
Beside the Spanish envoy, pray . . .
That lady in the red beret?'
'You *have* been out of circulation.
But I'll present you now with joy.'
'Who is she, though?' 'My wife, old boy.'

18

'You're married! Really?'—'On my honour.'
'To whom? How long?'—'Some two years since . . .
The Larin girl.'—'You mean Tatyana!'
'She knows you?'—'We were neighbours, Prince.'
'Well then, come on . . . we'll go and meet her.'
And so the prince led up to greet her
His kinsman and his friend Eugene.
The princess looked at him—serene;
However much the situation
Disturbed her soul and caused her pain,
However great her shock or strain,
She gave no hint of agitation:
Her manner stayed the same outside,
Her bow was calm and dignified.

19

It's true! The lady didn't shiver,
Or blush, or suddenly turn white . . .
Or even let an eyebrow quiver,
Or press her lips together tight.
Although Eugene with care inspected
This placid lady, he detected
No trace of Tanya from the past.
And when he tried to speak at last,
He found he couldn't. She enquired
When he'd arrived, and if of late
he'd been back home at his estate—
Then gave her spouse a look so tired,
He took her arm. She moved away . . .
And left Eugene in mute dismay.

20

Was this the Tanya he once scolded
In that forsaken, distant place
Where first our novel's plot unfolded?
The one to whom, when face to face,
In such a burst of moral fire,
He'd lectured gravely on desire?
The girl whose letter he still kept—
In which a maiden heart had wept;
Where all was shown . . . all unprotected?
Was this that girl . . . or did he dream?
That little girl whose warm esteem
And humble lot he'd once rejected? . . .
And could she now have been so bold,
So unconcerned with him . . . so cold?

21

He left the rout in all its splendour
And drove back home, immersed in thought;
A swarm of dreams, both sad and tender,
Disturbed the slumber that he sought.
He woke to find, with some elation,
Prince N. had sent an invitation.
'Oh God! I'll see her . . . and today!
Oh yes, I'll go!'—and straightaway
He scrawled a note: *he'd be delighted*.
What's wrong with him? . . . He's in a daze.
What's stirring in that idle gaze,
What's made that frigid soul excited?
Vexation? Pride? Or youth's old yen
For all the cares of love again?

22

Once more he counts the hours, pacing;
Once more can't wait till day is past.
The clock strikes ten: and off he's racing,
And now he's at the porch at last;
He enters in some apprehension;
The princess, to his added tension,
Is quite alone. Some minutes there
They sit. Eugene can only stare,
He has no voice. Without a smile,
And ill at ease, he scarcely tries
To answer her. His mind supplies
But one persistent thought the while.
His eyes retain their stare; but she
Sits unconstrained, quite calm and free.

23

Her husband enters, thus arresting
This most unpleasant tête-à-tête;
Eugene and he recalled the jesting,
The pranks and fun when first they'd met.
They laughed. Then guests began arriving.
And on the spice of malice thriving,
The conversation sparkled bright;
The hostess kept the banter light
And quite devoid of affectations;
Good reasoned talk was also heard,
But not a trite or vulgar word,
No lasting truths or dissertations—
And no one's ears were shocked a bit
By all the flow of lively wit.

24

The social cream had gathered gaily:
The nobly born and fashion's pets;
The faces one encounters daily,
The fools one never once forgets;
The aged ladies, decked in roses,
In bonnets and malignant poses;
And several maidens, far from gay—
Unsmiling faces on display;
And here's an envoy speaking slyly
Of some most solemn state affair;
A greybeard too . . . with scented hair,
Who joked both cleverly and wryly
In quite a keen, old-fashioned way,
Which seems a touch absurd today!

25

And here's a chap whose words are biting,
Who's cross with everything about:
With tea too sweet to be inviting,
With banal ladies, men who shout,
That foggy book they're all debating,
The badge on those two maids-in-waiting,*
The falsehoods in reviews, the war,
The snow, his wife, and much, much more.

. . . .

26

And here's Prolázov,* celebrated
For loathesomeness of soul—a clown,
As you, Saint-Priest,* have demonstrated
In album drawings all through town.
Another ballroom king on station
(Like fashion's very illustration)
Beside the door stood tightly laced,
Immobile, mute, and cherub-faced;
A traveller home from distant faring,
A brazen chap all starched and proud,
Provoked amusement in the crowd
By his pretentious, studied bearing:
A mere exchange of looks conveyed
The sorry sight the fellow made.

27

But my Eugene all evening heeded
Tatyana . . . only her alone:
But not the timid maid who'd pleaded,
That poor enamoured girl he'd known—
But this cool princess so resplendent,
This distant goddess so transcendent,
Who ruled the queenly Néva's shore.
Alas! We humans all ignore
Our Mother Eve's disastrous history:
What's given to us ever palls,
Incessantly the serpent calls
And lures us to the tree of mystery:
We've got to have forbidden fruit,
Or Eden's joys for us are moot.

28

How changed Tatyana is! How surely
She's taken up the role she plays!
How quick she's mastered, how securely,
Her lordly rank's commanding ways!
Who'd dare to seek the tender maiden
In this serene and glory-laden
Grande Dame of lofty social spheres?
Yet once he'd moved her heart to tears!
Her virgin brooding once had cherished
Sweet thoughts of him in darkest night,
While Morpheus still roamed in flight;
And, gazing at the moon, she'd nourished
A tender dream that she someday
Might walk with him life's humble way!

29

To love all ages yield surrender;
But to the young its raptures bring
A blessing bountiful and tender—
As storms refresh the fields of spring.
Neath passion's rains they green and thicken,
Renew themselves with joy, and quicken;
And vibrant life in taking root
Sends forth rich blooms and gives sweet fruit.
But when the years have made us older,
And barren age has shown its face,
How sad is faded passion's trace! . . .
Thus storms in autumn, blowing colder,
Turn meadows into marshy ground
And strip the forest bare all round.

30

Alas! it's true: Eugene's demented,
In love with Tanya like a boy;
He spends each day and night tormented
By thoughts of love, by dreams of joy.
Ignoring reason's condemnation,
Each day he rides to take his station
Outside her glassed-in entryway,
Then follows her about all day.
He's happy just to be around her,
To help her with her shawl or furs,
To touch a torrid hand to hers,
To part the footmen who surround her
In liveried ranks where'er she calls,
Or fetch her kerchief when it falls.

31

She pays him not the least attention,
No matter what he tries to do;
At home receives him without tension;
In public speaks a word or two,
Or sometimes merely bows on meeting,
Or passes by without a greeting:
She's no coquette in any part—
The *monde* abhors a fickle heart.
Onegin, though, is fading quickly;
She doesn't see or doesn't care;
Onegin, wasting, has the air
Of one consumptive—wan and sickly.
He's urged to seek his doctors' view,
And these suggest a spa or two.

32

But he refused to go. He's ready
To join his forebears any day;
Tatyana, though, stayed calm and steady
(Their sex, alas, is hard to sway).
And yet he's stubborn . . . still resistant,
Still hopeful and indeed persistent.
Much bolder than most healthy men,
He chose with trembling hand to pen
The princess an impassioned letter.
Though on the whole he saw no sense
In missives writ in love's defence
(And with good cause!), he found it better
Than bearing all his pain unheard.
So here's his letter word for word.

Onegin's Letter to Tatyana

I know you'll feel a deep distress
At this unwanted revelation.
What bitter scorn and condemnation
Your haughty glance may well express!
What aims . . . what hopes do I envision
In opening my soul to you?
What wicked and deserved derision
Perhaps I give occasion to!

When first I met you and detected
A warmth in you quite unexpected,
I dared not trust in love again:
I didn't yield to sweet temptation
And had, it's true, no inclination
To lose my hateful freedom then.
What's more: poor guiltless Lensky perished,
And his sad fate drew us apart. . .
From all that I had ever cherished
I tore away my grieving heart;
Estranged from men and discontented,
I thought: in freedom, peace of mind,
A substitute for joy I'd find.
How wrong I've been! And how tormented!

But no! Each moment of my days
To see you and pursue you madly!
To catch your smile and search your gaze
With loving eyes that seek you gladly;
To melt with pain before your face,
To hear your voice . . . to try to capture
With all my soul your perfect grace;
To swoon and pass away . . . what rapture!

And I'm deprived of this; for you
I search on all the paths I wander;
Each day is dear, each moment too!
Yet I in futile dullness squander
These days allotted me by fate . . .
Oppressive days indeed of late.
My span on earth is all but taken,
But lest too soon I join the dead,
I need to know when I awaken,
I'll see you in the day ahead . . . .

I fear that in this meek petition
Your solemn gaze may only spy
The cunning of a base ambition—
And I can hear your stern reply.
But if you knew the anguish in it:
To thirst with love in every part,
To burn—and with the mind each minute,
To calm the tumult in one's heart;
To long to clasp in adoration
Your knees . . . and, sobbing at your feet,
Pour out confessions, lamentation,
Oh, all that I might then entreat! . . .
And meantime, feigning resignation,
To arm my gaze and speech with lies:
to look at you with cheerful eyes
And hold a placid conversation! . . .

But let it be: it's now too late
For me to struggle at this hour;
The die is cast: I'm in your power,
And I surrender to my fate.

33

No answer came. Eugene elected
to write again . . . and then once more—
With no reply. He drives, dejected,
To some soirée . . . and by the door,
Sees *her* at once! Her harshness stuns him!
Without a word the lady shuns him!
My god! How stern that haughty brow,
What wintry frost surrounds her now!
Her lips express determination
To keep her fury in control!
Onegin stares with all his soul:
But where's distress? Commiseration?
And where the tearstains? . . . Not a trace!
There's wrath alone upon that face . . .

34

And, maybe, secret apprehension
Lest *monde* or husband misconstrue
An episode too slight to mention,
The tale that my Onegin knew . . . .
But he departs, his hopes in tatters,
And damns his folly in these matters—
And plunging into deep despond,
He once again rejects the *monde*.
And he recalled with grim emotion,
Behind his silent study door,
How wicked spleen had once before
Pursued him through the world's commotion,
Had seized him by the collar then,
And locked him in a darkened den.

35

Once more he turned to books and sages.
He read his Gibbon and Rousseau;
Chamfort, Manzoni, Herder's pages;
Madame de Staël, Bichat, Tissot.
The sceptic Bayle he quite devoured,
The works of Fontenelle he scoured;*
He even read some Russians too,
Nor did he scorn the odd review—
Those journals where each modern Moses
Instructs us in a moral way—
Where I'm so much abused today,
But where such madrigals and roses
I used to meet with now and then:
E sempre bene, gentlemen.

36

And yet—although his eyes were reading,
His thoughts had wandered far apart;
Desires, dreams, and sorrows pleading—
Had crowded deep within his heart.
Between the printed lines lay hidden
Quite other lines that rose unbidden
Before his gaze. And these alone
Absorbed his soul . . . as he was shown:
The heart's dark secrets and traditions,
The mysteries of its ancient past;
Disjointed dreams—obscure and vast;
Vague threats and rumours, premonitions;
A drawn-out tale of fancies grand,
And letters in a maiden's hand.

37

But then as torpor dulled sensation,
His feelings and his thoughts went slack,
While in his mind Imagination
Dealt out her motley faro pack.
He sees a youth, quite still, reposing
On melting snow—as if he's dozing
On bivouac; then hears with dread
A voice proclaim: 'Well then, he's dead!'
He sees forgotten foes he'd bested,
Base cowards, slanderers full-blown,
Unfaithful women he had known,
Companions whom he now detested . . .
A country house . . . a windowsill . . .
Where she sits waiting . . . waiting still!

38

He got so lost in his depression,
He just about went mad, I fear,
Or else turned poet (an obsession
That I'd have been the first to cheer!)
It's true: by self-hypnotic action,
My muddled pupil, in distraction,
Came close to grasping at that time
The principles of Russian rhyme.
He looked the poet so completely
When by the hearth he'd sit alone
And *Benedetta** he'd intone
Or sometimes *Idol mio** sweetly—
While on the flames he'd drop unseen
His slipper or his magazine!

39

The days flew by. The winter season
Dissolved amid the balmy air;
He didn't die, or lose his reason,
Or turn a poet in despair.
With spring he felt rejuvenated:
The cell in which he'd hibernated
So marmot-like through winter's night—
The hearth, the double panes shut tight—
He quit one sparkling morn and sprinted
Along the Neva's bank by sleigh.
On hacked-out bluish ice that lay
Beside the road the sunlight glinted.
The rutted snow had turned to slush;
But where in such a headlong rush

40

Has my Eugene directly hastened?
You've guessed already. Yes, indeed:
The moody fellow, still unchastened,
Has flown to Tanya's in his need.
He enters like a dead man, striding
Through empty hall; then passes, gliding,
Through grand salon. And on! . . . All bare.
He opens up a door. . . . What's there
That strikes him with such awful pleading?
The princess sits alone in sight,
Quite unadorned, her face gone white
Above some letter that she's reading—
And cheek in hand as down she peers,
She softly sheds a flood of tears.

41

In that brief instant then, who couldn't
Have read her tortured heart at last!
And in the princess then, who wouldn't
Have known poor Tanya from the past!
Mad with regret and anguished feeling,
Eugene fell down before her, kneeling;
She shuddered, but she didn't speak,
Just looked at him—her visage bleak—
Without surprise or indignation.
His stricken, sick, extinguished eyes,
Imploring aspect, mute replies—
She saw it all. In desolation,
The simple girl he'd known before,
Who'd dreamt and loved, was born once more.

42

Her gaze upon his face still lingers;
She does not bid him rise or go,
Does not withdraw impassive fingers
From avid lips that press them so.
What dreams of hers were re-enacted?
The heavy silence grew protracted,
Until at last she whispered low:
'Enough; get up. To you I owe
A word of candid explanation.
Onegin, do you still retain
Some memory of that park and lane,
Where fate once willed our confrontation,
And I so meekly heard you preach?
It's my turn now to make a speech.

43

'Onegin, I was then much younger,
I daresay better-looking too,
And loved you with a girlish hunger;
But what did I then find in you?
What answer came? Just stern rejection.
A little maiden's meek affection
To you, I'm sure, was trite and old.
Oh God!—my blood can still turn cold
When I recall how you reacted:
Your frigid glance . . . that sermonette! . . .
But I can't blame you or forget
How nobly in a sense you acted,
How right toward me that awful day:
I'm grateful now in every way. . . .

44

'Back then—far off from vain commotion,
In our backwoods, as you'll allow,
You had no use for my devotion . . .
So why do you pursue me now?
Why mark me out for your attention?
Is it perhaps my new ascension
To circles that you find more swank;
Or that I now have wealth and rank;
Or that my husband, maimed in battle,
Is held in high esteem at Court?
Or would my fall perhaps be sport,
A cause for all the *monde* to tattle—
Which might in turn bring you some claim
To social scandal's kind of fame?

45

'I'm weeping. . . . Oh, at this late hour,
If you recall your Tanya still,
Then know—that were it in my power,
I'd much prefer words harsh and chill,
Stern censure in your former fashion—
To this offensive show of passion,
To all these letters and these tears.
Oh *then* at least, my tender years
Aroused in you some hint of kindness;
You pitied then my girlish dreams. . . .
But *now*! . . . What unbecoming schemes
Have brought you to my feet? What blindness!
Can you, so strong of mind and heart,
Now stoop to play so base a part?

46

'To me, Onegin, all these splendours,
This weary tinselled life of mine,
This homage that the great world tenders,
My stylish house where princes dine—
Are empty. . . . I'd as soon be trading
This tattered life of masquerading,
This world of glitter, fumes, and noise,
For just my books, the simple joys
Of our old home, its walks and flowers,
For all those haunts that I once knew . . .
Where first, Onegin, I saw you;
For that small churchyard's shaded bowers,
Where over my poor nanny now
there stands a cross beneath a bough.

47

'And happiness was ours . . . so nearly!
It came so close! . . . But now my fate
Has been decreed. I may have merely
Been foolish when I failed to wait;
But mother with her lamentation
Implored me, and in resignation
(All futures seemed alike in woe)
I married. . . . Now I beg you, go!
I've faith in you and do not tremble;
I know that in your heart reside
Both honour and a manly pride.
I love you (why should I dissemble?);
But I am now another's wife,
And I'll be faithful all my life.'

48

She left him then. Eugene, forsaken,
Stood seared, as if by heaven's fire.
How deep his stricken heart is shaken!
With what a tempest of desire!
A sudden clink of spurs rings loudly,
As Tanya's husband enters proudly—
And here . . . at this unhappy turn
For my poor hero, we'll adjourn
And leave him, reader, at his station . . .
For long . . . forever. In his train
We've roamed the world down one slim lane
For long enough. Congratulation
On reaching land at last. Hurray!
And long since time, I'm sure you'd say!

49

Whatever, reader, your reaction,
and whether you be foe or friend,
I hope we part in satisfaction . . .
As comrades now. Whatever end
You may have sought in these reflections—
Tumultuous, fond recollections,
Relief from labours for a time,
Live images, or wit in rhyme,
Or maybe merely faulty grammar—
God grant that in my careless art,
For fun, for dreaming, for the heart . . .
For raising journalistic clamour,
You've found at least a crumb or two.
And so let's part; farewell . . . adieu!

50

Farewell, you too, my moody neighbour,
And you, my true ideal, my own!
And you, small book, my constant labour,
In whose bright company I've known
All that a poet's soul might cherish:
Oblivion when tempests flourish,
Sweet talk with friends, on which I've fed.
Oh, many, many days have fled
Since young Tatyana with her lover,
As in a misty dream at night,
First floated dimly into sight—
And I as yet could not uncover
Or through the magic crystal see
My novel's shape or what would be.

51

But those to whom, as friends and brothers,
My first few stanzas I once read—
'Some are no more, and distant . . . others.'*
As Sadi* long before us said.
Without them my Onegin's fashioned.
And she from whom I drew, impassioned,
My fair Tatyana's noblest trait . . .
Oh, much, too much you've stolen, Fate!
But blest is he who rightly gauges
The time to quit the feast and fly,
Who never drained life's chalice dry,
Nor read its novel's final pages;
But all at once for good withdrew—
As I from my Onegin do.

THE END

APPENDIX

EXCERPTS FROM *ONEGIN'S JOURNEY*

PUSHKIN'S FOREWORD

The last (eighth) chapter of *Eugene Onegin* was published separately with the following foreword:

The omission of certain stanzas has given rise on more than one occasion to criticism and jesting (no doubt most just and witty). The author candidly confesses that he has removed from his novel an entire chapter, in which Onegin's journey across Russia was described. It behoved him to indicate this omitted chapter by dots or a numeral, but to avoid ambiguity he thought it preferable to label as number eight, instead of nine, the final chapter of *Eugene Onegin*, and to sacrifice one of its closing stanzas:

> It's time: my pen demands a pillow;
> Nine cantos have I duly wrought,
> And now the ninth and final billow
> To joyful shore my bark has brought.
> All praise to you, O nine Camenae,* etc.

P. A. Katenin* (whose fine poetic talent in no way prevents him from being a subtle critic as well) has observed to us that this excision, though advantageous perhaps for the reader, is none the less harmful to the work as a whole, for it makes the transition from Tatyana the provincial miss to Tatyana the exalted lady too sudden and unexplained: an observation that reveals the accomplished artist. The author himself felt the justness of this reproach but decided to omit the chapter for reasons important to him, but not to the public. Some few excerpts have been published already; we insert them here, along with several other stanzas.

ONEGIN TRAVELS FROM MOSCOW
TO NIZHNI NOVGOROD

* * *

. . . . . .

. .   before his eyes
Makáriev Market* stirs and bustles,
A-seethe with plenty's wares and cries.
The Hindu's here—his pearls to proffer,
All Europe—specious wines to offer;
The breeder from the steppe as well
Has brought defective steeds to sell;
The gambler's here with dice all loaded,
With decks of cards of every type,
The landed gent—with daughters ripe,
Bedraped in dresses long outmoded;
All bustle round and lie like cheats,
And commerce reigns in all the streets

* * *

Ennui! . . .

ONEGIN DRIVES TO ASTRAKHAN,
AND FROM THERE TO THE CAUCASUS

* * *

He sees the wilful Terek* roaring
Outside its banks in wayward flow;
He spies a stately eagle soaring,
A standing deer with horns held low,
By shaded cliff a camel lying,
Circassian steed on meadow flying;
All round the nomad-tented land
The sheep of Kalmuk herdsmen stand,
And far ahead—Caucasian masses.
The way lies open; war has passed
Beyond this great divide at last,
Across these once imperilled passes.
The Kúra's and Arágva's banks*
Have seen the Russians' tented ranks.

* * *

And now his gazing eye discovers
Beshtú,* the watchman of the waste;
Sharp-peaked and ringed by hills, it hovers . . .
And there's Mashúk,* all green-encased,
Mashúk, the source of healing waters;
Amid its magic brooks and quarters
In pallid swarms the patients press,
All victims: some—of war's distress,
And some of Venus, some of Piles.
Within those waves each martyred soul
Would mend life's thread and make it whole;
Coquettes would leave their ageing smiles
Beneath the waves, while older men
For just one day seek youth again.

* * *

Consumed by bitter meditation,
Onegin, mid those mournful crowds,
With gaze of keen commiseration
Regards those streams and smoky clouds,
And with a wistful sigh he muses:
Oh, why have I no bullet's bruises?
Or why am I not old and spare,
Like that poor tax collector there?
Or why not crippled with arthritis,
The fate that Tula clerk was dealt?
And why—O Lord—have I not felt
A twinge at least of some bursitis?
I'm young and still robust, you see;
So what's ahead? Ennui, ennui! . . .

ONEGIN THEN VISITS TAURIS [THE CRIMEA]

* * *

A land by which the mind is fired:
Orestes with his friend here vied,*
And here great Mithridates* died,
And here Mickiéwicz* sang inspired,
And, by these coastal cliffs enthralled,
His distant homeland he recalled.

* * *

O lovely land, you shores of Tauris,
From shipboard looming into sight,
As first I saw you rise before us,
Like Cypris* bathed in morning's light.
You came to me in nuptial splendour;
Against a sky all blue and tender
The masses of your mountains gleamed;
Your valleys, woods, and hamlets seemed
A patterned vision spread before me.
And there where Tartar tongues are spoke
What passions in my soul awoke!
What mad and magic yearnings tore me
And held my flaming bosom fast!
But now, O Muse, forget the past!

* * *

Whatever feelings then lay hidden—
Within me now they are no more:
They've passed away or changed unbidden . . .
So peace to you, you woes of yore!
Back then it seemed that I required
Those desert wastes and waves inspired,
Those massive cliffs and pounding sea,
The vision too of 'maiden free,'
And nameless pangs and sweet perdition . . .
But other days bring other dreams;
You're now subdued, you vaulting schemes
Of youthful springtime's vast ambition,
And in this poet's cup of mine
I now mix water with my wine.

* * *

Of other scenes have I grown fonder:
I like a sandy slope of late,
A cottage with two rowans yonder,
A broken fence, a wicket gate,
Grey clouds against a sky that lowers,
Great heaps of straw from threshing mowers,
And 'neath the spreading willow tree—
A pond for ducks to wallow free.
The balalaika's now my pleasure,
And by the country tavern door
The peasant dance's drunken roar.
A housewife now is what I treasure;
I long for peace, for simple fare:
Just cabbage soup and room to spare.

* * *

The other day, in rainy weather,
As I approached the farm . . . Enough!
What prosy ravings strung together,
The Flemish painter's motley stuff!
Was I like that when I was tender,
Bakhchisarái,* you fount of splendour!
Were these the thoughts that crossed my mind
When, 'neath your endless chant I pined
And then in silence meditated
And pondered my Zaréma's* fate? . . .
Within those empty halls ornate,
Upon my trail, three years belated,
While travelling near that selfsame sea,
Onegin, pausing, thought of me.

* * *

I lived back then in dry Odessa . . .
Where skies for endless days are clear,
Where commerce, bustling, crowds and presses
And sets its sails for far and near;
Where all breathes Europe to the senses,
And sparkling Southern sun dispenses
A lively, varied atmosphere.
Along the merry streets you'll hear
Italian voices ringing loudly;
You'll meet the haughty Slav, the Greek,
Armenian, Spaniard, Frenchman sleek,
The stout Moldavian prancing proudly;
And Egypt's son as well you'll see,
The one-time corsair, Moralí*

* * *

Our friend Tumánsky* sang enchanted
Odessa's charms in splendid verse,
But we must say that he was granted
A partial view—the poet's curse.
No sooner here than he went roaming,
Lorgnette in hand and senses foaming,
Above the lonely sea . . . and then
With his enraptured poet's pen
He praised Odessa's gardens greatly.
That's fine of course, but all I've found
Is barren steppeland all around,
Though here and there much labour lately
Has forced young boughs, I must admit,
To spread their grudging shade a bit.

* * *

But where's my rambling story rushing?
'In dry Odessa'—so said I.
I might have said: 'Odessa gushing'
And even so have told no lie.
For six whole weeks it happens yearly,
On stormy Zeus's orders clearly:
Odessa's flooded, drowned, and stuck,
Immersed in thickly oozing muck.
In mud waist-high the houses snuggle;
On stilts alone can feeble feet
Attempt to ford the muddy street.
The coaches and the people struggle,
And then the bent-head oxen pant
To do what helpless horses can't.

* * *

But now the hammer's smashing boulders,
And soon with ringing slabs of slate
The salvaged streets will muster shoulders,
As if encased in armoured plate.
But moist Odessa, all too sadly,
Is lacking yet one feature badly:
You'll never guess . . . it's water-short!
To find the stuff is heavy sport . . .
But why succumb to grim emotion?
Especially since the local wine
Is duty free and rather fine.
And then there's Southern sun and ocean . . .
What more, my friends, could you demand?
A blessèd and most favoured land!

* * *

No sooner would the cannon, sounding,
Proclaim from ship the dawn of day
Than, down the sloping shoreline bounding,
Towards the sea I'd make my way.
And there, my glowing pipe ignited,
By briny waves refreshed and righted,
In Muslim paradise complete,
I'd sip my Turkish coffee sweet.
I take a stroll. Inciting urges,
The great Casino's opened up;
I hear the ring of glass and cup;
The marker, half asleep, emerges
Upon the porch, with broom in hand,
Where two expectant merchants stand.

* * *

And soon the square grows gay and vital.
Life pulses full as here and there,
Preoccupied by work . . . or idle,
All race about on some affair.
That child of ventures and finances,
The merchant to the port advances,
To learn the news: has heaven brought
The long-awaited sail he sought?
Which just-delivered importations
Have gone in quarantine today?
Which wines have come without delay?
And how's the plague? What conflagrations,
What wars and famines have occurred?
He has to have the latest word.

* * *

But we, we band of callow joysters,
Unlike those merchants filled with cares,
Have been expecting only oysters . . .
From Istanbul, the seaside's wares.
What news of oysters? Here? What rapture!
And off runs glutton youth to capture
And slurp from salty shells those bites
Of plump and living anchorites,
With just a dash of lemon flavour.
What din, debates! The good Automne*
From cellar store has just now come
With sparkling wine for us to savour.
The time goes by and, as it goes,
The bill to awesome stature grows.

* * *

But now blue evening starts to darken,
And to the opera we must get,
The great Rossini there to harken,
Proud Orpheus and Europe's pet.
Before no critic will he grovel,
He's ever constant, ever novel;
He pours out tunes that effervesce,
That in their burning flow caress
The soul with endless youthful kisses,
With sweetly flaming love's refrain,
A golden, sparkling fine champagne,
A stream that bubbles, foams, and hisses.
But can one justly, friends of mine,
Compare this do–re–mi with wine?

* * *

And what of other fascinations?
And what of keen lorgnettes, I say . . . ?
And in the wings . . . the assignations?
The prima donna? The ballet?
The *loge*, where, beautiful and gleaming,
The merchant's youthful wife sits dreaming,
All vain and languorous with pride,
A crowd of slaves on every side?
She heeds and doesn't heed the roses,
The cavatina, heated sighs,
The jesting praise, the pleading eyes . . .
While in the back her husband dozes,
Cries out from sleep *Encore!*—and then
Emits a yawn and snores again.

* * *

The great finale's thunder surges.
In noisy haste the throng departs;
Upon the square the crowd emerges,
Beneath the gleam of lamps and stars.
Ausonia's * happy sons are humming
The playful tune that keeps on drumming,
Against the will, inside their brains—
While I roar out the light refrains.
But now it's late. Odessa's dreaming;
The breathless night is warm and soft,
While high above the moon's aloft,
The sky all lightly veiled and streaming.
No stir disturbs the silence round,
Except the sea's incessant sound.

* * *

And so I lived in old Odessa . . .

EXPLANATORY NOTES

2 *Pétri . . . particulière*: the main epigraph to the novel, apparently written by Pushkin himself, translates roughly as follows: 'Steeped in vanity, he was possessed moreover by that particular sort of pride that makes a man acknowledge with equal indifference both his good and evil actions, a consequence of a sense of superiority, perhaps imaginary. From a private letter.'

dedication: The dedication was originally addressed to Pushkin's friend (and the first publisher of *Eugene Onegin*) P. A. Pletnyov (1792–1862). In later editions, the piece was retained as a kind of preface, but without the inscription to Pletnyov.

Chapter 1

5 *My uncle, man of firm convictions*: the novel's opening words mimic a line from the fable *The Ass and the Peasant* by Ivan Krylov (1796–1844): 'An ass of most sincere convictions.'

Ludmíla's and Ruslán's adherents: the author's address to his readers and references to other of his writings are devices used throughout the novel. The allusion here is to Pushkin's first major work, the mock epic *Ruslán and Ludmíla*.

noxious in the north: 'Written in Bessarabia' (Pushkin's note). A lightly veiled allusion to the poet's troubles with the court: a few poems of liberal sentiment and some caustic epigrams had incurred the wrath of the emperor, and as a consequence, in May 1820, Pushkin was required to leave St Petersburg for an unspecified term of exile in the south of Russia. He would not return to the capital for more than six years.

6 *Letny Park*: the Summer Garden, a public park situated along the embankment of the Neva and adorned with shade trees and the statues of Greek deities.

9 (9): here and elsewhere, numbers in parentheses indicate stanzas omitted by Pushkin in the published text.

10 *Faublas*: the hero of a novel by the French writer Louvet de Couvrai (1760–97). Abetted in the seduction of other men's wives by a rakish count, Faublas, it turns out, has seduced his accomplice's bride as well.

10   *Bolivár*: 'Hat à la Bolivar' (Pushkin's note). A wide-brimmed black top hat, named after the South American liberator, which was fashionable in both Paris and St Petersburg in the 1820s.

    Bréguet: an elegant pocket-watch made by the celebrated French watchmaker, Abraham Louis Bréguet (1747–1823).

11   *Talon's*: Talon was a well-known French restaurateur in St Petersburg.

    Kavérin: Pyotr Kaverin (1794–1855) was a hussar, man about town, and friend of Pushkin.

    comet wine: champagne from the year of the comet (1811), a year of especially good vintage.

    Strasbourg pie: a rich pastry made with goose liver, for which the French city is famous.

11   *Cleopatra . . . Phèdre . . . Moïna*: the heroines of various plays, operas, or ballets performed in St Petersburg at the time. The *Cleopatra* that Pushkin had in mind is uncertain; the *Phèdre* was either Racine's tragedy or an opera based on it; Moïna is the heroine of Ozerov's tragedy, *Fingal*.

12   *Enchanted land! . . . perfected*: the stanza evokes the Russian theatre around the turn of the century, when for the most part imitations of Corneille, Racine, and Molière prevailed. D. Fonvizin (1745–92), the most noteworthy of the playwrights mentioned, was the author of two successful satires, *The Minor* and *The Brigadier*. Y. Knyazhnin (1742–91), V. Ozerov (1769–1816), and P. Katenin (1792–1852) wrote Frenchified tragedies; A. Shakhovskoy (1777–1846) wrote equally derivative comedies. E. Semyonova (1786–1849) was an accomplished Shakespearian actress who performed in Russian dramas as well. Charles-Louis Didelot (1767–1837), French ballet master and choreographer, was associated with the St Petersburg ballet.

13   *Istómina*: A. I. Istomina (1799–1848). A celebrated ballerina who was a pupil of Didelot. She danced in ballets that were based on works by Pushkin, and early in her career the poet had courted her.

15   *Grimm*: Frédéric Melchior Grimm (1723–1807). French encyclopedist. In a note to these lines Pushkin quotes from Rousseau's *Confessions* on the encounter between the two men and then comments: 'Grimm was ahead of his age: nowadays, all over enlightened Europe, people clean their nails with a special brush.'

15 *Chadáyev*: the manuscript provides evidence for the name given here. Pyotr Chadayev (1793–1856) was a friend of the poet and a brilliant personality. Both fop and philosopher, he was the author of the famous *Lettres philosophiques*, of which only one was published in Russia during his lifetime. His work helped to precipitate, through its critique of Russian history, the great debate between the Westernizer and Slavophile camps of Russian thought. For the expression of his ideas, Chadayev was officially declared insane, although he continued to take an active part in Moscow social life.

22 *Say or Bentham*: the French economist Jean Baptiste Say (1767–1832) and the English jurist and philosopher Jeremy Bentham (1748–1832) were much discussed at the time in progressive circles.

Capricious . . . spleen: in a note to the stanza Pushkin comments archly: 'The whole of this ironical stanza is nothing but a subtle compliment to our fair compatriots. Thus Boileau, under the guise of reproach, eulogizes Louis XIV. Our ladies combine enlightenment with amiability, and strict purity of morals with that Oriental charm which so captivated Mme. de Staël.' See *Dix ans d'exil*.

25 *As . . . himself*: a mocking allusion to M. Muravyov (1757–1807) and his lyric poem 'To the Goddess of the Neva'.

26 *Brenta*: the river that flows into the Adriatic near Venice.

Albion's great and haughty lyre: the reference is to Byron's poetry.

shore: 'Written in Odessa' (Pushkin's note).

my Africa's warm sky: 'The author, on his mother's side, is of African descent. His great-grandfather, Abram Petrovich Annibal, in his eighth year was abducted from the coast of Africa and taken to Constantinople. The Russian envoy, after rescuing him, sent him as a gift to Peter the Great, who had him baptized in Vilno.' Thus Pushkin begins a rather lengthy note on the life of his African ancestor. The young man was subsequently sent abroad by Peter to study fortification and military mining. After a sojourn of some seven years in France, he was recalled to the service in Russia, where he had a rather chequered career as a military engineer. He was eventually made a general by the empress Elizabeth and died in retirement, in 1781, at nearly 90 years of age, on one of the estates granted him by the crown. The third of his eleven children (by a second wife) was the poet's maternal grandfather.

30 *sang the Salghir captives' praises*: the references are to the heroines
in two of Pushkin's narrative poems: the Circassian girl in *The
Caucausian Captive* and the harem girls in *The Fountain of
Bakhchisarai*. The Salghir is a river near Bakhchisarai, a Tartar
town and former residence of the Crimean khans.

Chapter 2

33 *O rus! . . . O Rus'!*: the epigraph employs a pun. The first 'O rus!'
(Horace, *Satires* 2. 6) means 'O countryside!'; the second invokes
the old and lyrical name for 'Russia'.

36 *corvée . . . rate*: the *corvée* was the unpaid labour that a serf was
required to provide to his master. Onegin, an enlightened squire,
has decided to improve the lot of his peasants by asking instead
for a small payment.

37 *Mason*: since Masonic organizations at the time were centres of
liberal thought, a provincial landowner would have considered the
member of such a group a revolutionary.

38 *That there exists . . . redeeming grace*: the last five lines of this
stanza, which give Lensky's views on the mission of poets, were
omitted by Pushkin from the final text, presumably because he
anticipated the censor's objection.

43 *passions*: the dangerous emotions or 'passions' refer here not only
to sensual love but also to feelings of enmity, jealousy, and
avarice.

46 *that name*: 'The most euphonious Greek names, such as,
for example, Agathon, Philetus, Theodora, Thecla, and so forth,
are used with us only among the common people' (Pushkin's
note).

50 *shaved the shirkers*: serfs who were chosen by their owners for
army service had their forelocks shaved for easy recognition.

52 *At Trinity . . . deserved*: lines 5–11 were omitted in all editions
during Pushkin's lifetime. On Trinity Day, the Sunday after
Whitsunday, people often brought a birch-tree branch or a
bouquet of field flowers to church. The tradition in some regions,
according to Vladimir Nabokov, called for the worshipper to shed
as many tears for his sins as there were dewdrops on the branch
he carried.

53 *Ochákov decoration*: a medal that commemorated the taking of the
Black Sea fortress of Ochakov in 1788, during the Turkish
campaign.

Chapter 3

55 *Elle . . . amoureuse*: 'She was a girl, she was in love.'

58 *A drink . . . coach*: in most editions the final six lines of this stanza are omitted.

59 *Svetlana*: the reference is to the heroine of a ballad by Vasily Zhukovsky (1783–1852), a talented poet and Pushkin's friend.

61 *Julie Wolmár*: the heroine in a novel by Rousseau, *Julie, ou La Nouvelle Héloïse*.

Malék-Adhél: the hero of *Mathilde*, a novel by Mme Cottin (1773–1807).

de Linár: a character in the novel *Valérie* by Baroness von Krüdener (1764–1807).

Clarissa: the heroine of Richardson's *Clarissa*.

Julia: again, the character from Rousseau's *Julie*.

Delphine: the heroine in a novel of the same name by Mme de Staël.

62 *The Vampire . . . Sbogar*: the Vampire is presumably from the 1819 tale of that name by John Polidori, Byron's physician. Melmoth is the hero of *Melmoth the Wanderer*, published in 1820 by Charles Robert Maturin. *The Corsair* is the poem by Byron. The legend of the wandering Jew was widely used by writers in the Romantic era. *Jean Sbogar* is the title of a short French novel published in 1818 by Charles Nodier. These are all works of Pushkin's own time, whereas Tatyana's reading comes from an earlier generation; only in Chapter Seven will she discover Byron in Onegin's abandoned library.

70 *The Good Samaritan*: a Moscow literary journal, actually called the *Well-Intentioned* (Blagonamerennyj).

71 *Bogdanóvich*: I. F. Bogdanóvich (1743–1803): a minor poet and translator from the French. His narrative poem *Dushen'ka* (Little Psyche) exerted some influence on the young Pushkin.

Parny: Evariste-Désiré de Parny (1753–1814). French poet famed for the elegance of his love poetry. His *Poésies érotiques* influenced Russian poetry of the late eighteenth and early nineteenth centuries.

Bard of The Feasts: the reference is to Evgeny Baratynsky (1800–44), a friend of Pushkin's and a fellow poet. His elegy *The Feasts* was written in 1820, while its author was serving in the ranks in Finland, after having been expelled from military school for theft. Set in a gloomy Finland, his poem evokes a happier time with poet-friends in the Petersburg of 1819.

72 *Freischütz*: the reference is to the overture from *Der Freischütz*, an opera by Carl Maria von Weber (1786–1826).

Chapter 4

83 *La morale . . . choses*: 'Morality is in the nature of things.'

96 *Tolstoy*: Count F. P. Tolstoy (1783–1873): a well known and fashionable artist.

97 *No madrigals . . . flows:* the octave of this stanza exhibits a rare divergence from the usual pattern: like the Italian sonnet, it employs but two rhymes in the eight lines and thus provides a rather pleasing accompaniment to a discussion of poetic form.

   Yazýkov: N. M. Yazýkov (1803–46): a minor poet and acquaintance of Pushkin.

   trumpet, mask, and dagger: emblems of the classical drama.

   odes: for Pushkin the term 'ode' suggested bombastic and heavy pieces in the eighteenth-century Russian manner; his own preference was clearly for the romantic 'elegy', by which term he would have described any short contemplative lyric. The mock debate conducted in this and the following stanza reflects an actual dispute between the 'archaists' and 'modernists' of Pushkin's day.

98 *The Other*: the allusion is to *Chuzhoi tolk* (Another's View), a satire on the writers of odes by I. Dmitriev (1760–1837).

99 *36*: this stanza appeared only in the separate edition of Chapters 4 and 5.

100 *Gulnare's proud singer*: Byron, in *The Corsair*.

102 *Pradt*: Dominique de Pradt (1759–1837): a prolific French political writer.

103 *Hippocrene*: a fountain or spring on Mount Helicon in Boeotia, sacred in Greek mythology to the Muses.

104 *Aï*: or Ay; a champagne whose name derives from a town in the Marne district of northern France.

   entre chien et loup: dusk, or the time of day 'between the dog and the wolf' (i.e., when the shepherd has difficulty in distinguishing between the two).

106 *Lafontaine's*: August Lafontaine (1758–1851). A German writer, author of numerous novels on family life.

Chapter 5

110 *Another bard . . . shade*: 'See *First Snow*, a poem by Prince Vyazemsky' (Pushkin's note). Prince Pyotr Vyazemsky (1792–1878), poet, critic, and wit, was a close friend of Pushkin. He appears in the novel by name in Chapter 7, stanza 49.

bard of Finland's maid divine!: 'See the descriptions of the Finnish winter in Baratynsky's *Eda*' (Pushkin's note).

112 *'The Kitty's Song'*: at Yuletide, and especially on Twelfth Night, several traditions for fortune-telling were observed by women and girls (particularly among the common people). The shapes taken by molten wax or lead when submerged in water were read as prophetic, and so-called 'dish divining songs' were sung. In the latter case, girls would place their rings in a covered bowl of water before singing carols. At the end of each song, a ring was drawn at random, and its owner would deduce some portent or meaning from the kind of song just sung. Tatyana's song on this occasion is a portent of death, whereas 'The Kitty's Song', which girls prefer, is a prophecy of marriage.

113 *trains a mirror . . . nearer*: training a mirror on the moon was another method of divination, the reflected face of the man-in-the-moon supposedly revealing to the enquiring maiden her future husband.

'Agafon': by asking the name of the first stranger she encountered, a girl hoped to learn the name of her future fiancé. The name that Tatyana hears, Agafon (from the Greek 'Agathon'), sounds particularly rustic and old-fashioned, and therefore comic, to a Russian ear.

conjure all night through: another device for discovering one's husband-to-be: conjuring up his spirit at an all-night vigil.

Svetlana: the heroine of Zhukovsky's ballad. In the poem, when Svetlana conjures her absent lover, he carries her off to his grave. Fortunately, Svetlana's terrors remain only a dream.

Lel: supposedly a pagan Slavic deity of love; more likely (according to Nabokov) merely derived from the chanted refrain of old songs (e.g., the *ay lyuli lyuli* of many Russian folk-songs).

119 *Martýn* Zadéck: the name, evidently a fabrication, appears as the author of several collections of prophecies and dream interpretations, published both in Russia and in Germany.

120 *Malvina*: a novel by Mme Cottin (1773–1807).

Two Petriads: heroic poems on Peter the Great, several of which were in circulation at the time.

Marmontel: Jean François Marmontel (1723–99), French encyclopedist and short-story writer.

121 *But lo! . . . the sun*: 'A parody of some well-known lines by Lomonosov' (Puskin's note). The crimson hand of Aurora (deriving of course from the Homeric 'rosy-fingered dawn') appears in several odes by M. V. Lomonosov (1711–65), scientist and poet and the founder of Moscow University.

Buyánov: Mr Rowdy, the hero of a popular and racy poem by Pushkin's uncle, Vasily Pushkin; thus, playfully, Pushkin's cousin. The names given to the other guests are also traditionally comic ones: Pustyakov (Trifle), Gvozdin (Bash), Skotinin (Brute), Petushkov (Rooster).

122 *Réveillez-vous, belle endormie*: Awaken, sleeping beauty.

Tatyaná: Triquet pronounces Tatyana's name in the French manner, with the stress on the last syllable.

124 *a lavish pie*: the Russian *pirog*, a meat- or cabbage-pie.

Zizí: Evpraksia Wulf (1809–83), who as a young girl lived near Pushkin's family estate at Mikhailovskoe and with whom he flirted when confined there in 1824. Pushkin became her lover briefly in 1829. Writing to a friend in 1836 from Mikhailovskoe on his last visit there, he recalls her as 'a formerly half-ethereal maiden, now a well-fed wife, big with child for the fifth time'.

127 *Albani's glory*: Francesco Albani (1578–1660): Italian painter much admired in the eighteenth and early nineteenth centuries.

Chapter 6

131 *La sotto . . . dole*: 'There, where the days are cloudy and short | Is born a race that has no fear of death.'

135 *Regulus*: the Roman general Marcus Atilius Regulus, who, upon his capture by the Carthaginians, was sent to Rome to deliver harsh terms for peace; whereupon he returned to his captors as he had promised and was executed.

Véry's: Café Véry, a Parisian restaurant.

141 *Delvig*: Baron Anton Delvig (1798–1831), minor poet and one of Pushkin's closest friends, his classmate at the Lyceum in Tsarskoe Selo.

144 *Lepage's deadly pieces*: Jean Lepage (1779–1822), famous Parisian gunsmith.

Chapter 7

158 *Lyóvshin's crew*: students of works by Vasily Lyovshin (1746–1826), author of numerous tracts on gardening and agriculture.

165 *iron bust*: A statuette of Napoleon.

166 *The bard of Juan and the Giaour*: Byron.

173 *Autómedons*: Autómedon was the charioteer of Achilles in the *Iliad*.

174 *Petróvsky Castle*: the chateau not far from Moscow where Napoleon took refuge from the fires in the city.

179 '*Archival dandies*': young men from well-connected families who held cushy jobs at the Moscow Archives of the Ministry of Foreign Affairs.

    Vyázemsky: Prince Pyotr Vyazemsky (1792–1878), friend of Pushkin.

180 *Grand Assembly*: the Russian Assembly of Nobility, a Moscow club for noblemen.

Chapter 8

185 *Lycée*: the lyceum established by Alexander I at Tsarskoe Selo for young aristocrats. Pushkin attended the boarding-school there between 1811 and 1817, and to the end of his life remained deeply attached to his friends of those years. It was at the lyceum that he composed his first poems.

    Derzhávin: Gavrila Derzhávin (1743–1816): the most outstanding Russian poet of the eighteenth century. In the year before he died, Derzhávin attended a school examination at which the 16-year-old Pushkin recited one of his poems, which the old man praised.

186 *Lenore*: the heroine of the romantic ballad by Gottfried Bürger (1747–94).

    Tauris: an ancient name for the Crimea. Pushkin's visit to the Crimea and his earlier stay in the Caucasus (to which he refers in a line above) were commemorated in two of his so-called 'southern' poems, *The Prisoner of the Caucasus* and *The Fountain of Bakhchisarai*.

    Nereids': sea-nymphs, daughters of the sea-god Nereus.

187 *sing the savage steppe*: an allusion to the narrative poem *The Gypsies*, yet another of Pushkin's southern works.

my garden: Pushkin's country place at Mikhailovskoe, to which he was confined by the government from August 1824 to September 1826 and where he resumed work on *Eugene Onegin*.

Demon of my pen!: a reference to his poem 'The Demon', in which he speaks of having been haunted in his youth by an 'evil genius', a spirit of negation and doubt who mocked the ideals of love and freedom.

191 *Chatsky*: the hero of Griboedov's comedy *Woe from Wit* (1824). Chatsky, after some three years abroad, turns up on the day of a party at the Moscow house of the girl he loves.

Shishkov: Admiral Alexander Shishkov (1754–1841), the leader of the Archaic group of writers, was a statesman and publicist who attacked both Gallicisms and liberal thought in Russian letters.

192 *epigram of style*: an allusion to some possible epigrammatic play on the word 'vulgar' and the last name of Faddei Bulgarin (1789–1859), a literary critic and notorious police informer who was hostile to Pushkin.

Nina Voronskáya: an invented name for a stylized society belle. Russian commentators on the poem have suggested various real-life prototypes.

197 *badge on those two maids-in-waiting*: a court decoration with the royal initials, given to ladies-in-waiting of the empress.

Prolázov: the name (derived from *prolaza*, roughly 'sycophant' or 'social climber') appears only in posthumous editions. According to Nabokov it was often attached to ridiculous characters in eighteenth-century Russian comedies and in popular pictures.

Saint-Priest: Count Emmanuel Sen-Pri (1806–28), the son of a French *émigré* and a noted caricaturist.

204 *Gibbon and Rousseau ... Fontenelle he scoured*: the listing device is a favourite of Pushkin's. Besides Rousseau, this catalogue of Onegin's reading includes: Edward Gibbon (1737–94), the English historian; Sébastien Chamfort (1740–94), French writer famous for his maxims and epigrams; Alessandro Manzoni (1785–1873), Italian novelist and poet of the Romantic school; Johann Gottfried von Herder (1744–1803), the German philosopher; Mme de Staël (1766–1817), the French writer (whose novel *Delphine* was listed earlier as one of Tatyana's favourites); Marie F. X. Bichat (1771–1802), French physician and anatomist,

the author of *Recherches physiologiques sur la vie et la mort*; Simon Tissot (1728–1797), a famous Swiss doctor, author of the treatise *De la santé des gens de lettres*; Pierre Bayle (1647–1706), French philosopher, author of the famous *Dictionnaire historique et critique*; Bernard Fontenelle (1657–1757), French rationalist philosopher and man of letters, author of *Dialogues des morts*.

205 *Benedetta*: 'Benedetta sia la madre' (Blessed be the mother), a popular Venetian barcarolle.

Idol mio: 'Idol mio, piu pace non ho' (My idol, I have peace no longer), the refrain from a duet by Vincenzo Gabussi (1800–46).

212 '*Some are no more, and distant . . . others*': though probably written in 1824, these lines were taken almost immediately as an allusion to Pushkin's friends among the executed or exiled Decembrists (participants in the ill-fated revolt of December 1825).

Sadi: the thirteenth-century Persian poet.

Appendix

215 *Camenae*: water-nymphs identified with the Greek Muses.

Katenin: Pavel Katenin (1792–1853). A minor poet and critic, whose *Recollections of Pushkin* were published in the twentieth century.

217 *Makáriev Market*: a famous market fair held in midsummer in the town of Makariev, to which it moved in 1817 from Nizhni Novgorod.

218 *Terek*: a river in the Caucasus.

Kúra's and Arágva's banks: refers to two mountain rivers in the Caucasus.

Beshtú: (or Besh Tau): a five-peaked mountain eminence in the northern Caucasus.

Mashúk: one of the peaks in the northern Caucasus.

219 *Orestes with his friend here vied*: a reference to the tale of Orestes and his friend Pylades, who argued over which of them would be sacrificed to the goddess Artemis, each wishing to die in the other's place. In the end both escaped, along with the temple priestess, who turned out to be Iphigenia, Orestes' sister.

Mithridates: King of Pontus, who in 63 BC, after being defeated by Rome, ordered one of his soldiers to kill him. Pushkin visited his alleged tomb while travelling in the Crimea in 1820.

219 *Adam Mickiéwicz*: Polish national poet (1798–1855), who spent almost five years in Russia, where he made the acquaintance of Pushkin. His visit to the Crimea in 1825 provided material for his *Crimean Sonnets*.

220 *Cypris*: Venus or Aphrodite.

221 *Bakhchisarái*: the reference is to a fountain in the garden of the Crimean Khan's palace. See Pushkin's narrative poem 'The Fountain of Bakhchisarai'.

Zaréma: the jealous wife of the Khan, one of the heroines in Pushkin's poem 'The Fountain of Bakhchisarai'.

222 *Moralí*: (or Moor Ali): apparently a Moorish seaman or pirate, whom Pushkin met during his stay in Odessa.

Tumánsky: a minor poet who served along with Pushkin as a clerk to the governor of Odessa.

225 *Automne*: César Automne, a well-known restaurateur in Odessa.

226 *Ausonia*: Italy.

The Oxford World's Classics Website

www.worldsclassics.co.uk

- Information about new titles
- Explore the full range of Oxford World's Classics
- Links to other literary sites and the main OUP webpage
- Imaginative competitions, with bookish prizes
- Peruse *Compass*, the Oxford World's Classics magazine
- Articles by editors
- Extracts from Introductions
- A forum for discussion and feedback on the series
- Special information for teachers and lecturers

www.worldsclassics.co.uk

American Literature

British and Irish Literature

Children's Literature

Classics and Ancient Literature

Colonial Literature

Eastern Literature

European Literature

History

Medieval Literature

Oxford English Drama

Poetry

Philosophy

Politics

Religion

The Oxford Shakespeare

A complete list of Oxford Paperbacks, including Oxford World's Classics, OPUS, Past Masters, Oxford Authors, Oxford Shakespeare, Oxford Drama, and Oxford Paperback Reference, is available in the UK from the Academic Division Publicity Department, Oxford University Press, Great Clarendon Street, Oxford OX2 6DP.

In the USA, complete lists are available from the Paperbacks Marketing Manager, Oxford University Press, 198 Madison Avenue, New York, NY 10016.

Oxford Paperbacks are available from all good bookshops. In case of difficulty, customers in the UK can order direct from Oxford University Press Bookshop, Freepost, 116 High Street, Oxford OX1 4BR, enclosing full payment. Please add 10 per cent of published price for postage and packing.